LIKE SILK BREATHING

CAMILLE DUPLESSIS

Copyright ©2022 by Camille Duplessis

Published by Oliver-Heber Books

0 9 8 7 6 5 4 3 2 1

❧ Created with Vellum

For N.

AUTHOR'S NOTE

As in many fairy tales, the circumstances here are somewhat ominous, but like many romances, they conspire to result in a happy ending. *Like Silk Breathing* depicts grieving after a bereavement, mental illness, and alcohol addiction. I don't want to catch any readers off-guard by not mentioning it right at the start. I know they can be difficult things to encounter, so please be aware they're here. They're not graphically portrayed, and you're always welcome at my table if you resonate with anything these characters think or go through.

On the note of complex emotions and experiences, Mary Oliver and Louise Glück's poetry were among the inspirations for this book and (soon) series. Additionally, there is so much queer history in Britain beyond the obvious and mainstream. I encourage you to read widely on the subject.

This is a story of joy and quiet rebellion, and I hope you love it.

1

LATE DECEMBER, 1886

Cromer

His physician kept telling him to think of other things, and to devote himself to his work or take a holiday somewhere more permissive like France. "You need to allow yourself to grieve," Dr. Jones had said. "That might mean leaving the grief to one side for a little while. Go take in some art, some flowers." He was encouraging in a quiet, bracing manner and he surely meant to help within the dire circumstances.

"How, exactly, do I put grief down long enough to smell a rose?" Paul had replied.

He'd known Mr. Paul Apollyon for a few years and kept him as a patient for the last two, and more importantly, he always offered decent counsel without any overtones of moralism.

But Alistair was dead and Paul could no more think of other things than he could turn into a sparrow and fly to the supposedly more permissive continent. Such alchemy would be the only way he could afford to holiday anywhere anyway. He wished he could be something else, anything else, a bird would suit him, because his mind was fixed on one harrowing reminiscence above others.

The insistent repetition of mundane affairs could not break the memory's hold on him. Peculiar stillness was the first thing Paul noted when he woke next to Alistair and idly touched his chest in their moonlit bedroom. He'd done it so many times before, reached out when he'd woken, and Alistair took his hand and kissed the back of it or the inside of his palm.

Paul hadn't thought of death because what kind of man would?

Then he realized there couldn't be an alternative. It wasn't that Alistair was cold, for he wasn't yet. But his chest wasn't rising or falling the way it should, and his pine scent was no longer in the air. It wasn't a real scent from a soap or cologne. Paul sensed it only in the most abstract manner and had long known he could only discuss the predilection with a select few – he'd never talked to his own brother about it, and they discussed almost every subject, including some of the most taboo.

This one was not exactly taboo though. It was too singular to be, for while Paul had learned there were others who shared his abilities, he still didn't think there was a sizable number. Along with discerning scents that were not there, he sometimes dreamed about things that later happened, a dubious talent that had unnerved him as a boy. Having little bearing on his adult life besides how it impacted him internally, it was all good material for fairy stories.

So he generally kept it to himself, having no desire to be evaluated by doctors with their modern specialisms or sent away for his own good. He already trifled with one such attribute that might result in either of those things and it was very earthly, so he did not want to own another that did not promise love or pleasure.

Even though the vitalizing pine had dissipated by the time Paul was lightly touching Alistair at half-past three in the morning, he'd gone to bed smiling, joking, loving. This was what Paul had to reckon with, his greatest friend's sudden being and not-being, until he looked in a small, battered diary and found Alistair's son's information. Alistair was older than him by twelve or so years, being months away from fifty when he passed, and had a grown son, James.

He'd talked about him often, written at least fortnightly, and never gave up hope that even though his father was an unspeakable, James might reply. After Paul contacted him, he had to reckon with James wanting nothing to do with him or The Shuck, the pub Paul and Alistair had run for several years.

He tried to tell James his father never wanted to cause him pain and wished to be involved in his life, but James harbored a resolute sourness toward the situation.

Death, apparently, was the thing to catch his attention. His mother had died before Paul met Alistair, so perhaps it followed that he mourned deeply. He had neither parent left. The heart always held more than one emotion, and grief and bitterness were bedfellows in James's: he wouldn't tell Paul where Alistair was to be buried. In short, he disapproved of his father's choices and evidently didn't want Paul to be able to visit him.

Old Fisk, the undertaker, was decent about everything: he readied Alistair for a journey somewhere undisclosed, with a charge, of course, but he'd still done it and never passed a demeaning comment. He knew their arrangement. And someone who judged it could never have been so gentle when they explained they were going to prepare the body for transport and an eventual burial.

Paul wondered how many people outside of his regular patrons might have gleaned the truth of it all. Some must have, like Mr. Mills, a wealthy merchant who always donated money to the old veterans. His son was clandestinely *involved* with Paul's nephew, Silence – who went by Tom, understandably, because his father's idea of wit had taken the form of an unwieldy family name—or so the wagging tongues said.

Where his heavily-named nephew was concerned, Paul tried to stay reserved due to some fear he'd influence him in a bad direction. Now sixteen, Tom showed signs of being worrisomely similar. Paul was much less concerned about his arrant interest in men and far more alarmed that he seemed to possess comparable preternatural instincts to his own. They'd never talked about it, but he could see them in his old-soul hazel eyes and shamefaced body language.

The preternatural could run in families, after all.

Loving men probably didn't. But for him to possess both traits struck Paul as rather too much for one person to bear, and he'd know.

While he had not thought so before Alistair did not wake up next to him, he now felt Tom was uniquely predestined for misery and if he could discourage him from colliding with this destiny, he would. Especially when one of the best outcomes was having to outlive the person one loved.

That tax seemed much too high.

~

"I DID ALWAYS like this particular view, Mr. Apollyon," said Mrs. Lloyd.

Alistair's body left The Shuck for good after resting in the first-floor back parlor that faced the sea, which Paul kept as his private parlor. On that day, the beautiful Mrs. Lloyd had come to join him upstairs with a pot of tea, and a chipped vase of winter blooms, and a slightly mashed cake.

Once one of the best-paid courtesans in the area, she was presently his housekeeper and a local purveyor of confections. It was neither her age nor some new moral disinclination that kept her from her prior profession, but instead one bad hip and two bad knees. Mr. Lloyd, apparently, was not and had never been a hinderance to her particular source of generous income. He hadn't minded it in the least. But as a retired hostler, he understood the effect of one bad hip and two bad knees, and was quite happy to have her home more often.

Paul eyed the cake with mild amusement. Even if his own feelings could be identifiable right now, anything but numbness was largely foreign. But, he felt vague glee. "The view may be lovely, but that looks terrible," he said.

"It tastes much better than it looks. Mr. Lloyd let the cat knock it from the table. Thankfully, it was covered, or we would be picking who knows what out of the top, there."

"I wish you'd bring the cat here instead of a cake." He and Alistair had kept a grizzled polydactyl cat several months ago, but when she passed on to wherever good cats ended up, he hadn't bothered to find another. He'd liked Sally so much that any other cat just felt like a disrespectful replacement.

At the moment, he was starting to reconsider his

stance on a new cat. He hadn't even slept in his own bed for days, electing to sleep downstairs on a sofa he favored, and imagined he might benefit from a soft living creature especially if he couldn't have an extended holiday in Nice or Paris.

"She isn't allowed out of doors, otherwise I might. But there are too many folks coming and going, opening the main door of course and being careless. I would hate for her to stray where she shouldn't."

Like the dear soul she was, she put the plate complete with squished cake on the table he'd placed back on the Persian rug only after they'd taken Alistair out in a box. He hadn't bothered trying to follow or pry for details because James had threatened some kind of *action*, so he only knew that Alistair was destined for the north somewhere.

James liaised with Fisk after exchanging a letter with Paul, who tried to deduce where his father might be laid to rest using only James's address and things Alistair often mentioned about his son. Edinburgh was most probable, as it was where he resided. Fisk had to know more than he said, but likely did not wish to aggravate matters further by supplying particulars that were not his to give. And James was not the friendliest person toward anyone in Cromer, as though it were to blame for the circumstances.

Paul could understand it given the situation, even if he didn't like it.

Rather than reply to Mrs. Lloyd's statement about the cat, he said, apropos of nothing she'd actually said and more in respect of why she'd called, "I almost had him buried here, but then I thought of how he tried to keep writing his son and wondered if he'd hate me forever if I kept him to myself." He smirked at her.

Several people had called on him within the last

week, and his cadre of regular patrons had been in the taproom, but she was one of the few he gladly trusted.

"I don't think The Shuck could handle a ghost," he said, "but I must confess I would welcome the prospect for me. I could learn to enjoy being haunted."

"I wonder if Benson could confine a specter to your flat."

She did not know his true profession, but everyone gossiped and aside from the parochial propensity for blether, Benson did look eccentric. He often wore certain intricate sigils entwined with chains or cords or ribbons and kept his hair tangled and unfashionably long. In addition to all of that, he dressed himself in clothes that looked like either rags or a theatrical costume meant to evoke a mendicant.

Though he had a dear brother in Norwich and both were in possession of reliable if modest pensions, he gave the appearance of being unmoored and unkempt. Local children were prone to calling him "Merlin," which was not far from the truth of it.

Benson knew about both Paul and Paul's theories about Tom, but he was a curious case and had approached Paul about it: being a self-proclaimed witchhunter, he said he was uniquely attuned to them, descended from a long line of witches with a knack for gleaning the invisible undercurrents of internal and preternatural states. Benson said it was often like witnessing invisible, vividly shaded threads connecting people to their objects of desire or disdain. There could even be threads between them and loved ones or enemies. Paul could not envision any of this, but was open to the possibilities.

According to Benson, he was a witch. So was Tom.

They were good friends and had been since Paul

helped him resole his best pair of boots even *after* Benson had started asking rather strange personal questions like, *Do you happen to dream of things before they come?*

First, Paul assumed he was under the influence of something or other, then over time understood Benson was in earnest and trying to draw him out as a kindred soul.

The Apollyon family had always told yarns about relatives rumored to be witches, but they were just that to everyone: stories told with a smile and strong cup of tea in hand. After all, old and no-one-remem-bered-how-many-greats Granny Alexandra wasn't truly a sea witch, she was only a woman whose bones hurt when the weather was inclement. But it was great fun to think about it.

The stories were just stories to *almost* everyone, anyway.

Not Paul, though he'd decided early to stop talking about his experiences with knowing what someone would say before they said it, or dreaming of things a few days before they happened. Benson actually said he was probably more of a seer than a witch, but in today's age with its emphasis on rationality and evidence, he'd surely be treated for madness no matter what he was called.

And if he was any good at being a seer, surely he wouldn't have been so surprised by Alistair's death.

Surely he would have known about it before it happened, if he had any talent worth having.

"I'm not certain spirits and seances are his calling, but in Alistair's case, I do wish he could," said Paul. Alistair would be a tender ghost, he was sure of it. Not that he should *want* a ghost or think about his former lover *being* a ghost. What a ghastly thing to contemplate. He had been trying to read too many books to distract himself of late. None of the words registered for long, of course, but he did attempt to give himself something else to think about.

Out of politeness, he took some of the sad cake.

It collapsed and congealed like paper in rain as he chewed. Under other circumstances that did not involve the sudden death of his heart's companion, it would have been excellent cake, he was positive. His own skewed sense of taste must be sabotaging the innocent treat even if it had also been marginally smushed through a feline mishap.

"I am sorry, Mr. Apollyon."

"You really may call me Paul," he said, after he'd swallowed his bite. "Have I not said?"

"Oh, you have. But it would never do if a patron overheard."

Paul grunted in reply. Cromer and Overstrand did contain droves of people who observed the utmost in propriety to the point of ridiculousness. Again he thought of Mr. Mills and his ilk. He was the sort of ridiculously teetotal, proper man who clashed with some humble folks, yet he seemed extremely interested in aiding certain charitable endeavors. Like the veterans' causes.

Guilty conscience, I'd guess.

Maybe it was belated guilt passed through generations, for the Mills were known to have been beastly witch-hunters in their time. They were not like Benson, who was just a witch for hire when one got right down to it: he had the integrity to admit he wasn't unlike the folks his forbearers had procured and tortured. He turned his own preternatural talents in a different direction and chose never to harm. A nebulous distinction separated them, really, and even rarer individuals like selkies were supposedly not so distant from their witch and witch-hunter cousins. Paul had heard more about selkies than any other creatures except for the shuck, but he'd neither met a selkie – to his knowledge – nor really seen a shuck.

Mrs. Lloyd said, and he'd no notion if she'd spoken of anything else while he was musing and hoped he had not missed much, "Will you tell the younger Mr. Apollyon the truth of it? Your nephew, of course, not your brother. The very youngest." She was so fond of the quiet rapscallion, who was almost an outright copy of his father at the same age. Family resemblance was strong between the three of them. Often, when Tom was there to visit, an incomer or visitor would assume he was Paul's son.

"Which truth?" Paul was fond of him too, though it was difficult to express and becoming harder by the day to try. Besides, he suspected Tom already knew about him and Alistair.

If he couldn't guess on his own, he certainly might have heard some of the regulars passing remarks. Innocent ones, to be sure, for Paul was fortunate to be accepted despite the religious and civic attitudes toward men like him, but some remarks were still made.

It might have been because he didn't want to, but Tom was one of the people he could rarely read. He'd never dreamt about him, either. Benson asserted this was because like might repel like, but Paul could not have a strong opinion on the why of the matter when he'd never confirmed if they were indeed *like*. Science had no way of testing any of their theories, anyway, so he left well enough alone and kept his eye on more concrete matters like what kind of whisky and brandy patrons seemed to like best, or how to get the best price on flour.

"Any of it. All of it." Mrs. Lloyd was not fully aware of Paul's talents, but she did call him uncanny.

He knew she knew more than she ever let on, but having been a paramour for hire meant one would be an expert in reading people and keeping information to oneself.

"I don't think he needs to know."

She pursed her lips in tacit disapproval. "Doesn't he?"

I don't know how to explain that I can't handle the responsibility of telling him.

And so, he didn't, for the shame would be too heavy for him to bear. He let her pour tea to go with the cake and resolved to keep his peace on the matter. Alistair might have suggested otherwise, but Paul would try to keep his own counsel, now.

2

LATE DECEMBER, 1900

Cromer

Tom knew Paul would kill him for drinking on the job.

Nobody would trust a drunk proprietor because one would hope those who purveyed lodgings were sensible enough to keep them in good order. Supposedly, this was true. But Tom knew because he *was* a drunk proprietor that at least a few people were willing to trust one, namely him, because they hadn't realized he was under the influence of drink in the first place.

If Paul was well enough to come downstairs and upbraid him, he'd be dead as an effect of the lecture. But luckily—no, unluckily—his uncle's health presently suffered, even if life hadn't taken much else from him. It hadn't touched his livelihood or his assets.

Life *had* taken the one thing Paul seemed to want, Alistair, who'd seemingly vanished when Tom was sixteen. He was thirty now and no more knowledgeable about the matter. Eyeing the dark bottle he had in hand, Tom thought of the proprietor's flat upstairs, filled with expensive things that would have been the height of taste and fashion fourteen years ago.

Dust doesn't augment the value of anything. Gives it a gothic atmosphere, perhaps. He quite liked the gothic novels, the romances, the genres of historical literature that read more like ghost stories or fairy tales and were said by some to rot the mind. Maybe they did.

If dust added value and not atmosphere, Paul would be the wealthiest person in the county. The anniversary was today. Each year meant more dust and less festive cheer.

Paul had probably accumulated so much dust it wasn't clear how he could move about in his own lodgings.

Tom took a drink. Whatever it was, this came from Toothless Rob down the road and had been recommended by Benson, their resident drunkard besides him who kept nattering about a spell on The Shuck. The stuff didn't just burn, it also took away one's sense of smell before taking everything else along with it, which he wanted. Logic, discomfort, misery, joy. He was always trying to dampen what he felt and sensed, and had done so for years.

"Good morning, dear," said Mrs. Lloyd.

He looked from the worn but polished bar top to her face. He had already noticed her signature feeling well before he saw her. Everyone had one, a sensation, a phantom smell, sometimes a color that might loom for his eyes alone. It made many of his waking moments something of a hell, even if poets went on about synesthetic qualities.

"Starting early, are we?" She nodded to the bottle.

He chuckled. "Today is always difficult."

"You needn't take on Mr. Apollyon's difficulties as your own, you know."

"Mrs. Lloyd, I don't try and he still manages to make them my own."

Paul was a good person, kind to everyone but him. He seemed to rouse a kind of galling darkness, a deep well of not abuse, never abuse, but calm distain. Nothing he did could be done to his uncle's full satisfaction.

Well, the joke was precisely that until Mother asked—or perhaps begged, he wasn't sure—her brother-in-law to give Tom work. Tom did not want to be a proprietor. He'd gone instead to be a dock worker, then a fisherman, and for the most part, he did all that quite well. Well enough for his mother's husband to deem him unfit to work in their inn, anyway. *Their inn.* Even though it was completely her inn because it had originally been his father's. He did suspect there was more to it than Mother speaking to Paul, but no one ever told him what.

Mrs. Lloyd tutted and opened the curtains opposite him. He winced at the December light that reflected off the sea.

"Your father, God rest him, had such a tempering influence on this period."

"I wish he could, now."

"Oh, indeed." Mrs. Lloyd began to dust the windowsills. During the low season, everything seemed to collect more dirt.

While the taproom stayed busy throughout the year, the rooms above it might go empty. They couldn't compete with The Cliftonville or The Red Lion for notoriety or popularity, and they never tried to be stylish, but they managed all the same. In the end, there were their loyalists, he supposed. His father's inn in Norwich worked in tandem with The Shuck, too, and now that Mother was managing things, trade was very brisk.

"Better brothers you couldn't find," said Mrs. Lloyd. "Even with your father going to Norwich and Paul staying here to see to The Shuck."

Tom had trouble imagining Paul happier. Their own relationship, such as it was, felt obligatory, though he wished it didn't and had often wondered how to repair it.

He sipped, watching as Mrs. Lloyd moved to the second large window. They needed to replace these curtains. The oxblood was far too somber for an establishment by the sea, even if it was called The Shuck. The rather mordant name wasn't its original one, but had come from an incredibly drunk patron who swore on his wife's honor he'd seen the black shuck in an upper floor window of the pub.

The black shuck had been, in fact, a greatcoat precariously draped over a chair. Likewise, the wife's honor was not very strong. Alistair, being neither from Norfolk nor a cautious man, suggested they rename the pub.

"Really?" Tom hadn't seen them together much. But Mother had once told Tom the same.

She really was to be thanked for his role working here. Without her intervention, Tom was certain he would still be working whatever odd jobs crossed his path and fishing or laboring between those. Although he did not consider it beneath him to do so at all, the self-imposed lack of routine—and often, expected income—was hell on his nerves.

Then again, so was feeling out of place wherever he went.

But he might as well stay put. People seemed to respect that more.

Mrs. Lloyd nodded. "Paul, I mean to say, Mr. Apollyon, he was always the more cautious one despite being the older of the two. A shy sort of child, I'd imagine, although I didn't know them as children. Your father could draw him out, that's for certain."

"I do believe you could call him by his given name." Amused, Tom scribbled a note in the ledger before him. He was, despite being distracted by any person-specific color or smell that drifted into his path, quite good at keeping the pub. He'd been around them all his life. The Shuck in the summer and sometimes the spring, and his father's for the rest of the year.

If he'd been working here when Alistair had actually gone, perhaps he'd know more of the matter. He'd been told and he'd heard it said that the man just decided to return north to his grown son. But the decision could not have been a happy one, for Paul always became sullen for at least a fortnight during the festive season.

There were also no letters, no attempts at reconnecting even as peers or colleagues. He was old enough now to understand what that signified and even had his own example of a lover gone badly. With a shake of his head, he dusted the thought of David from his mind. He had not really thought of him in months, and certainly had not before returning to live here. Too much unfinished business was there.

"It would not do if a patron overheard," Mrs. Lloyd said.

"We have none. I don't even know why I'm downstairs." When things were leaner, they just took lodgers and became a boardinghouse of sorts. Mrs. Lloyd was well-suited to it, and they knew the men who presently resided in two of the rooms. Benson had one and the second was rented to a somber fellow called Jack who had come from Great Yarmouth several years prior.

"I try to stay in the habit."

"Very assiduous of you." Tom hesitated. Then he asked, "What do you know about today?" She had been working for the family for years and she was an astute listener, though less of a gossip in the sense that she did not spread what she heard. But she seemed to radiate so much uncertainty after being asked the question that Tom attributed the sudden onslaught of feeling to his amber bottle of mysterious liquor rather than admit he'd caused her discomfort.

Instead of putting it down, he took another drink.

She opened her mouth, paused before speaking, then said, "He was not the same after."

Disappointed, for this was not anything new to him, Tom said, "No, well, I imagine that is true."

After a longer pause, Mrs. Lloyd said, "You must not repeat anything I say to you."

He had been childish at the time, far too busy neglecting his responsibilities to pay attention to the uncle who was rarely kind to him anyway. But he had thought of himself as observant up until that point. It had all taken him directly to the only conclusion his young mind could make, which was precisely that his uncle was *like him*. He'd never had the courage to ask, but he'd thought Alistair, who kept the pub alongside Paul, was the likeliest candidate.

Now, he was certain of it. "I won't."

"Thank you. To be fair, I'm not at all certain it is my place to be telling you this. But I'm sure your mother is quite busy, these days." She had ceased her straightening and dusting. Not generally a trepidatious person, she stood still without any nervous tells, looking squarely at Tom. He gently brandished his bottle at her.

Despite her outward composure, there was still something about her demeanor, her person, that made the air roil for him.

"Have some of this, then," he said.

"I should not. I don't trust Rob."

"Neither do I," said Tom, but he grinned, then drank.

She sighed. "I don't know why he never wanted to speak to you about it."

"My uncle?"

"Yes."

"Go on, please."

"But you would not have seen him stepping out because he did not wish to compromise his trade. Or his life."

Frowning, Tom knew he was not too obtuse or drunk to miss the implication. Still, for politeness' sake, he said, "Was she an actress? A woman of ill-repute? Come on, even then, that would not have been so *terribly* scandalous. He's a man."

"No."

Tom shook his head and gave up his pretense at a decent misunderstanding. "I understand you."

"I do not think there is anything wrong with it, mind you," she said, firmly, clutching her dust rag like the hilt of a rapier, almost daring Tom to challenge her assertion. He did not want to.

He did, however, find it daunting himself, and not because he felt it was wrong. "Neither do I," he said. "But whether or not we do, it is illegal."

"Just so."

Many things Tom had an affinity for were dubiously legal or illegal. He bit at his own lip, trying to clear his head of memories that he only ever revisited in the dark when alone: conversations best had in the sanctum of loud pubs or secluded boats, sunlight on warm skin. A friend, David, who'd studied at Cambridge and was no longer a friend at all, but someone whose name he did not want to speak or think. Some dangers were delicious.

"Any reason given as to why he left, then?" It seemed hallowed and daring to say *he.*

"Well," said Mrs. Lloyd. She added, after a considerable pause, "I truly thought your mother would have it out of Paul, but she never did."

It only took him the fraction of a moment to know she was lying, and the lie irritated him. "So he keeps that flat. . ." He tipped his chin toward the ceiling. "Like a shrine. Like he's bloody—pardon—like he's Miss Havisham without the dress." Had Paul been warmer to him and had Mrs. Lloyd not lied, he might have aimed for a less snide tone. It was not that he wished suffering upon his uncle so much as he was tired of his curiosity being dodged.

Besides, today was a dark, inky day inside his own mind. *He* is *leaving you this place.* A very small, clear voice of reason dropped through the ink like a rivulet of milk in hot tea.

"It is possible that he believes the moment he changes anything, the more tangible the loss will be."

"How can it be any more tangible? Someone is gone. Absence is tangible."

"You'd best not have any more of that." Mrs. Lloyd glanced at the bottle. Tom set it down. "How about some breakfast?"

"Breakfast would be lovely, Mrs. Lloyd."

"Do not take on so much of his foul temper," she said. The benevolence in her voice made him cringe.

Where the air had just been roiling, it was now warm and calm.

He blinked. "I assure you, the only foul temper I have taken on is my own. I know my own mind."

Whatever his mind was, its penchants for sensing things that were not physical and preferring the whimsical to the practical were enormously grating. He looked like he should be residing in a remote house on the moors or captaining a boat. A lover had once said he was the absolute image of the green man, and Tom replied he had no use for cathedral bosses. But if he recalled correctly, they'd both been three pints into the evening and disinterested in discussing the nuances of either mythology or church architecture.

At the moment, his mind was preoccupied with the fact that his uncle was a confirmed bachelor, not in the sense of being alone, but in the more colloquial one. It was apparent that had Paul inferred the similarities between himself and even a young Tom, which could account for his standoffish behavior.

It had, after all, intensified only after they all found out Alistair had left him. But if Mrs. Lloyd was lying about something, his mother might be, too. Father had never been a good liar, though, which gave Tom some comfort because if he'd known anything more, what he knew most likely would have surfaced before his death.

But it did not have to be so bleak.

At least, Tom wished it did not have to be.

He distantly recalled his mother explaining how Paul had been cohabitating and it was no longer the arrangement, and even hearing about cohabitating outside of marriage was not as shocking as it might have been in some families. They simply were not so conservative. That it was a man and not a woman did perhaps change things, but he wondered if Mother had minded. Likely not, he felt. She did not mind him, after all.

"Your own temper is not so bitter as this," said Mrs. Lloyd. She smiled and patted his hand before quitting the taproom, off to make him breakfast as though he stood a chance of consuming it like a reasonable creature.

Reasonable creatures, though, did not sense phantom colors or smells when a person entered the room, or feel things that were not theirs to feel. As he tipped the bottle toward his lips, he also knew they did not inebriate themselves into near oblivion.

They did not need to trick everyone into believing they were ordinary.

3

If only Mrs. Lloyd was correct that his own temper was not *so bitter as this*.

Even that morning it had been eating at him, the gnawing agitation that something was not enough, something was uncanny and out of place, and *something* was him. *He* was uncanny and out of place.

Well, now he was drunk and wanted to die, neither of which was an unfamiliar state. He seemed to vacillate between one or the other without fail, and it was his damned intrusive senses and their onslaught that goaded him to either extreme. Without them, he might be prone to dark moods but still manage to appear normal. But *with* them, with all the added perceptions of what was not there, he was done for. It seemed his life was dominated by sensing things that were not truly reality.

It's a decent night to die on the beach, thought Tom, looking up at the heavy and luminous moon.

He had been thinking about Paul all day, especially after speaking with Mrs. Lloyd. What a lonely existence his uncle had. And he couldn't stand feeling like the inevitable would come, that he'd be heartbroken by something—someone—or his own mind would prove unreliable, forever manipulating him into melancholy or elation.

He would rather his heart gave out, like Father's.

But Mother would be devastated when they found his body. If they found it at all. The tide and all the mysterious creatures in the sea could do such damage to a man.

"Evening." A new presence came closer to him and he turned. This complicated his plans. If he'd been as keenly aware of everything unseen as he normally was, it would have struck him that someone else was nearby. But he was distracted by the surf and moonlight, trying to reckon how to turn turmoil into harmony and telling himself it was only possible through death.

"I know that look," said the man.

Tom shook his head. "What look?" He disregarded the warmth the man radiated and the alien feeling he brought to his surroundings. It was unlike anyone else's invisible mark, something Tom was certain he hadn't encountered at so close a distance.

He seemed familiar but Tom could not place him. "Wait until you're sober," he said. "Or at least until after the new year has dawned."

"Pardon?" Tom scowled. He had chosen this nook of the beach because unlike so many others, it wasn't busy, and it certainly wasn't busy in the small hours of the morning. It was removed enough from the inns and the pubs and any activity that might be happening at the moment, aboveboard or unsavory. Importantly, it was also a place where no one, even someone very skilled with a lifeboat, could reach him. "What business is it of yours whether I'm sober or not?"

Part of Tom's resolve chipped away when the

stranger smiled. There was promise in that smile. "If you're going to cast yourself into the sea," he said, "wait until you're not pickled by whisky."

"It's not whisky." Tom realized who he was, now, a secretary whom David had employed. While he had never been to The Shuck, Tom had noticed him in passing at his favorite bookseller's last week. It had been hard not to, for he was all angular beauty. Supposedly, he and David ventured here to Cromer together, according to local natter.

Even though Tom could place the man in his relation to another, he did not know his name. "I don't know what it is, actually, Mr.—"

Gently, he said, "Mr. Theodore Harper. Theo. You can call me Theo."

Several waves came and went as Tom gathered his thoughts. Theo seemed well-dressed in the moonlight, though it was hard to tell for certain, and he could not be past the middle of his third decade.

"Your eyes speak of mischief," said Tom. "Carry on with your walk and let me die in peace."

Theo laughed and Tom was displeased it wasn't a scathing chuckle. Then, at least, he could be indignant. Theo said, "I don't think this method of dying could be considered peaceful."

"Drowning? No." All anyone knew about drowning came from people who had not died, and he'd experienced a few situations where he'd not been able to surface before his lungs burned. The sensation was anything but peaceful. "But it's cold enough that I shouldn't be able to fight it long."

"Been around a lot of drownings, then?"

Tom scoffed at this impudent stranger who took very late nighttime promenades and apparently chuckled in the face of not only death, but melancholy too. "More than I would have liked." Before he could stop himself, he added, "I was a fisherman. And did some work on the docks."

"What are you, now?"

"A landlord, or a proprietor, or—no, I am about to end myself." Tom glanced at the water, which was like mercury under the wind and hardly welcoming.

"Why? And that's not what you are." Theo was hardly an inch shorter than him and stood far too close. He had also given his Christian name, and not only his Christian name, but also a pet name. Proximity probably did not signify anything improper under the circumstances, but that might have. "Neither is 'fisherman' or 'landlord,' really."

Tom began to laugh as he finished the sentence. He had not come out here to be lectured on philosophy by an impish, dashing stranger. He had chosen the time specifically for its remoteness to anyone respectable. If, of course, a drunkard could choose much with any sensible intent. "Very well. I am a failure."

Let Theo grapple with that for a moment.

He didn't take more than half of a moment to grapple with anything. "And that's why you're here."

"Why are you here?"

"The cold doesn't get to me, and I think the full moon is lovely."

"At two hours past midnight," said Tom, unconvinced.

"Aye, well, clouds kept it hidden."

Tom gazed at him, open-mouthed. Then he said, "Oh." That was true. It had been overcast in the evening.

"I think if you were going to cast yourself into the sea, you would have done it already."

Theo's amusement spurred Tom. Although it still

didn't seem to be of the scathing variety, he could not abide the empathy.

Nor could he take the soft tone like it was meant for a lover, and the implication that Theo had been in a situation like this, too, and all one had to do was weather the storm until it passed.

"I think clothes on shall do," Tom said. He had not, mercifully, been witness to *so* many drowning victims. Three, overall, and each in winter. All were inevitable because clothing weighted the victims, wool and leather becoming shackles to the sea floor until, days later, the bodies surfaced.

Theo eyed him rather impassively for a man who'd introduced himself in a familiar way and kept giving pronouncements on things like death and the moon's beauty. "Dead weight."

"What, nothing about the moon, then?" Tom asked, intending to be spiteful.

Theo only removed his hat and combed his fingers through dark hair, appearing thoughtful.

"I thought not," said Tom. Seized by the need to do something intimate in return for the intimacy of Theo's intervention, he reached for his own throat and unhooked a chain. He gathered both it and its pendant into the palm of his hand.

Theo watched the movements with marked curiosity.

"Here," Tom said. "For your trouble."

"It is no trouble."

"I'm sure it will be if you linger to watch my head disappear in the surf. Visibility is good, as you noted." Tom's hand was still outstretched. He bobbed it gently. "Go on."

Theo took the pendant without looking at it.

Had Tom been sober, he thought the warmth of his fingers might have been enough to make him stay. *Tonight.* But there was no telling what tomorrow would be like, or the day after. *Maybe you should just focus on the tonight and the next tonight one by one.*

No, nothing crucial could be so incremental.

Then Theo's hand closed around the pendant. "What is it?"

Tom said, "It's St. Julian. My grandmother gave it to me years ago."

"She argued with God," said Theo. "Julian did. Not your grandmother, of course. I'm sure she was a lovely person."

Tom smiled. Gran had not taken many of her life's difficulties with grace. She had been a lovely person indeed, but she did not suffer quietly and probably would have argued with anyone, God, saint, or mystic included.

"I'm not arguing. He's already won this altercation."

Leaving aside, of course, that God wasn't strictly relevant to his beliefs where he had them. He did not see how any god could actually be interested in his life, given how what he could sense and feel seemed far from godly. No loving deity and certainly not one he'd wish to follow would create him to feel so restless, either.

Theo pressed his lips together in a rueful, closed-mouth smile and said nothing as Tom started toward the water. Tom wished he would, but he didn't know what he'd wish to hear spoken. Still, Theo did not disappoint, at the last.

"What's your name?" The words carried over the rushing swells.

Without turning his body, Tom said over his shoulder, "Silence Apollyon. I'll dispense with the 'Mr.' given the circumstances, and it *is* truly Silence. But people usually call me Tom."

ilence? Theo thought.

On the contrary, he was quite talkative in a grim sort of way.

Saying so would probably not be well-received.

"What kind of name is Silence?" Theo had a plan, but it didn't involve trying to stop Tom from attempting what he so clearly thought he had to do. There was likely no way for Theo to overpower him, for Tom was a little bigger and indeed moved like a man who had made his living casting nets, climbing rigging, and doing all the assorted things a laborer might do. Which was to say, he most likely had a deceptive reserve of strength.

Anyway, Theo was at his best in water, which was where Tom would soon be. *The timing will be delicate.* He frowned. Wait too long, and he wouldn't be able to find him. Try too early, and he'd be able to fend Theo off before he had the chance to do any good. But he *was* intoxicated, which was in Theo's favor.

If he even noticed, an intoxicated man would rationalize a seal helping him back to land as the stuff of an addled mind, and Theo knew that as a person, he'd stand the same chances as Tom of drowning. He might withstand the cold longer, but in the end, the result would be the same.

Tom had his feet in the waves, now, but he shouted, "Puritan."

"It's almost 1901! How the hell do Puritans come into anything?" Theo could not help but chuckle through his yell. He carefully put the chain he'd just been given about his neck. The metal was still warm and the clasp was tricky, but he managed.

"The year does not change my ancestry, does it?"

Theo came closer to the waves, waiting. He said, "I suppose not."

"My mother thought I would be a girl. Sadly for her, I only share the same preferences as many girls." Tom was now up to his knees.

Theo had thought the man might be a fellow un-speakable of the Wilde sort, if one could or should make any assumptions of a stranger who was so obvi-ously planning to do himself in. Other than, of course, that particular one.

"They had only chosen the one name, which in retrospect seems a bit silly," Tom added.

While most would consider Tom an almost rugged example of a man, Theo knew better than to believe appearances dictated preferences. But only partially familiar with the tenets of Puritans from some travels to Boston, he said, "How is something like that sup-posed to be a girl's name?"

"Traditionally, it just is. I don't know." The water came to Tom's upper thighs, and his voice was starting to tremble a little from the cold. "They're all named after... Christ alive, that's cold... virtues and qualities, aren't they?"

He didn't know. "And your father? What does he think about this?"

"He was a wonderful man, in point of fact. He thought it was a pretty name for anyone, and a little bit of a joke, because apparently. . ." Tom trudged a few more steps until he was up to his waist. "*Jesus Christ and all the saints.* Apparently, I was a very loud infant. I cried. Shouted. Often."

Theo was willing to assert that Tom had not quite noticed he was being followed. "That does not seem to have changed."

The remark earned a short laugh and Theo warmed when he heard it. Tom said, "No. I can be vociferous when I put my mind to it."

A wave crashed against Tom, coming up to his nose.

Perhaps I won't have to change at all. The chill hadn't started to affect him just yet. He supposed shifting didn't matter if he was about to rescue someone. And the ends justified the means, possibly. . . but being just a man rather than a seal would simplify other things. He wouldn't have to explain as much should Tom be lucid enough to recall a seal being his savior.

Maybe changing *should* be a last resort. Anyone who couldn't was dubiously trustworthy until proven otherwise. He thought, or suspected, Tom might be one of the ones he could trust, but there was no way to be certain under the circumstances.

He chewed at his lip, evaluating his options.

The least of his concerns were he'd have to find a new hat; he was preparing to say good-bye to the one that had been on his head. It was still on the beach, but he'd dropped it thoughtlessly in the tide's path. Shifting conserved his clothes, though no one could tell him how or why, and he should have left it on. The future might be full of scholars who could explain it. A great many things had changed in his lifetime alone.

Theo shook his head to clear it and kept his eyes on Tom, whose posture sagged as he was battered by waves over his head. His own hat had been lost.

Even when he was markedly human, Theo had a better sense of the currents and their strength than most people. He relaxed and allowed his feet to rise from the sea floor. They were heavy in his shoes, but it couldn't be helped. *Go on, then, go under and I can get to dragging you out.*

It did not, until that immediate moment, occur to him that Tom probably wouldn't be grateful for the rescue. It only gave Theo a second of pause, for he did not know if he had the resolve to just let the man die.

It took several more moments and deep breaths against the wind and tide for Tom to fall. When he did, Theo was ready and dove without hesitation. It was too dark to see once Tom drifted underwater, so Theo groped around like they were playing a game of Blind Man's Bluff while he swam against the swells, trying to stay near where Tom slipped away.

He grazed a bit of hair. When he tried to grab it, it slipped away. *How long can he hold his breath?* Sailors and fishermen were like anyone else, bound by the same natural laws. Unless they were like him. He paused infinitesimally. *Never heard of a selkie fisherman.* But then, he'd neither asked any of the ones he'd met nor paid enough attention to them to tell.

He felt hair slip past him again and plunged forward, rewarded by a body colliding with his legs. "You'll not be dragged out to sea today, Mr. Drunkard." Taking a breath, he ducked under a wave and took a firm grasp on an arm, paying little care to how rough he was. One could mend an arm only if one was brought ashore.

Tugging, bringing his other hand into contact with Tom's opposite shoulder, Theo brought him into a more upright position, as upright as a man shocked by cold and lack of breath could be in deep water, and pushed his head toward the moon's ominous glow.

5

T heir return to shore did not take long. But by then even Theo, not always one for consuming drink, longed for a fireside whisky. He should probably get them indoors, and there was unquestionably more than one public house or hotel within walking distance. For safety's sake, he might have to choose the closest.

Heaving for breath, Theo hauled Tom onto land. Carefully, he let Tom's head rest on the inside of his arm.

The ethics of what he'd just done, namely save a life, seemed straightforward. They seemed, in a word, good. He toyed with the medal he'd been given. Mother Julian wouldn't want him to let Tom die.

In a manner he'd learned from another fisherman, he leaned forward and listened. Felt for any breath. Winter was treacherous, for a man could go into shock much faster and might not inhale much water before his breath stopped.

But Tom wasn't breathing. Gently, Theo readjusted his own arm and let him rest directly on his back, and tilted his lolling head forward just a little.

"There are some even now who call this witchcraft.

I don't know if they mean it." He didn't know why he was speaking to a man who could not hear him, but at the least, talking gave him some illusion of control. Sopping wet, shaking from the cold, he began fast, hard chest compressions. "There are still others who find it disgusting for what comes next."

Theo found nothing disgusting about placing his mouth upon another man's, although he indubitably preferred it under more sensuous circumstances. Carefully, he made sure Tom's chin was slightly lifted, then pinched his nose shut.

Sighing, ignoring the thought of how inviting Tom's lips might have been if they weren't on a beach with one of their lives at stake, he sealed Tom's mouth with his. Blew into it and ignored the strong taste of what had to be homemade spirits, concentrated instead on the lingering warmth.

He had seen it work after one breath.

He had seen it work after two, or several.

Delivered promptly enough, it could be instrumental in whether or not someone lived. He did not have the luxury of contemplating if he would be successful, but he did not have to wonder for long.

Tom began to cough so violently it jostled their faces apart. Theo took a deep breath and sat back, still shaking, waiting for an onslaught of angry recriminations. They might come after Tom had voided the seawater from his lungs. It didn't sound like he had swallowed much, but even a little could induce retching. Theo reflected, trying to decide what had motivated him to save a stranger from death.

Rather than deliberate too deeply, he decided the next course of action would be to get Tom inside.

"W-w-what the hell did you do?"

There it was, the anger. "You. . . you've lived to try to hurt yourself again," said Theo.

"That wasn't your choice to make!"

"You did speak a lot for someone who wanted to die."

"I was—am—drunk!"

"That's never a time to make enormous decisions."

Tom coughed too much to make a reply. Theo placed a hand on his arm as he hauled himself into a sitting position, and he did not bat it away. Then a curious thing happened: there was a flaring of heat under Theo's palm, accompanied by a quick and fluid awareness that aside from his fury, Tom was almost awed. This wasn't just an inference. Theo knew. He felt it nearly as if it were his own emotion until it seemed to mellow and recede from his sense of awareness.

He'd never experienced anything like it and being of a curious disposition, he regretted their present circumstances. They weren't the right ones for further inquiry.

"You may not know it since we haven't been properly introduced, but that *is* how I have made most of my decisions. I'm drunk as often as I am sober. More often, honestly." Tom wheezed and spat into the sand next to him. "Trivial or momentous, my choices are made with the help of some liquid that burns."

Soon he would begin to shiver, Theo surmised. For now, he was protected from the temperature by all the things a body did after it had a great scare. "We need to get you indoors, Mr. Drunkard."

Tom looked at him. "We?"

"Y-yes."

Now Tom looked at his arm, then at Theo's palm

on his arm. "You're trembling." He looked up at Theo's face and said, "Your teeth are chattering."

"Yes. It's winter, we're drenched, and we're on a beach." Being more of a seal than a man did little good if one didn't utilize the prior quality. He was cold as any other person would be on a beach in late December, but he could withstand it for longer. He plucked at his coat.

"I'm not," said Tom.

"You are indeed on a beach, soaked through to the skin, and it is still winter," Theo said with the barest of arch tones. He tried to speak clearly.

"Trembling. I'm not trembling." Tom shook his head, but Theo would have made an obvious joke again if it meant seeing the quick glint in Tom's eyes. Everything out here was cast in grays, including their features, but something told Theo that most of Tom's coloring was comprised of autumnal forest shades. Browns and hazels and dark greens.

"You are," said Theo. "And the longer we sit, the more obvious it will be that you want to be indoors with two fingers of something very strong while you sit before a fire. Perhaps while waiting for a warm bath." Theo let his hand fall from Tom, who kept his eyes on his face. "How is your arm?"

Wiggling first his left, then his right, Tom winced the more he moved the latter. "They both seem to work."

"The right was what I grabbed to keep you from being swept out. There are stories about this coast, you know. Wouldn't want you to be trapped with a lot of temperamental spirits."

"P-plenty of stories. There are always plenty of stories about coasts, though."

"Yes, well. I'm interested in a particular genre," said Theo.

"What kind?"

Theo stood, satisfied Tom was functional if not fully sound in mind or body, and said, "Ghost stories." He nodded toward the water. "Among others, I've heard all about the village that's flooded out there, not so very far away. And I know about Old Shuck, of course... I've never seen a great black dog along the beaches, though."

With a frown, Tom said, "Shipden. That's the village. Bizarre to think a whole village is under the water, now, because any of this might end up there by that logic." Then he scowled. "You are trying to distract me."

Smiling, but only just, Theo extended a hand. "Is it working?"

Clearly of an obstinate bent, Tom said, "No." Nonetheless, he took Theo's hand and allowed him to help pull him to his feet. On almost level footing, they were still of a close height. Tom was not much taller than him at all. Their shoes squelched as they straightened and took their first halting steps.

"Your shoes may survive," said Theo, "but only if you remove them soon and place them near a hearth.. . not too close. Then again, you are probably well aware of how to care for them. I don't suppose your feet stayed dry all the time you were working in your previous endeavors."

Tom stared at him and Theo experienced a shining moment of purely wanting to kiss him. Truly kiss him, not return his breath. What was worse, he registered small tells that Tom wanted to, as well. The list of his body toward Theo, the almost imperceptible quickening of his breath.

"How much experience do you have with, ah, wet, sodden shoes?" Tom said.

"Plenty." Rather than kiss a killjoy of a young man, he started them up the beach toward the road. If Tom asked what kind of experience, he would have to be creative in his rejoinder, but he'd had years of practicing his creative wordplay. His survival depended upon it and he'd been taught since childhood that a bit of prevention went a long way to secure safety. His father had instructed him well in how to obfuscate and how to hide in plain sight.

The only thing Father had in common with seal folk in stories was his belief in hiding. He had not left his ordinary lover after some extraordinary struggle. She, Theo's mother, had left him, deriding his mild nature for what she believed was cowardice. She'd never discovered who or what he was; she'd never known about his skin.

She'd never had the chance to wonder why he kept it so close. In the end, her inferences that he was nothing but a disappointment were a boon. There'd been no dramatics of the mythical variety, no lost skin and therefore no endeavor to find and secure it. Everything that had happened to his mother and father could have happened to anyone's mother and father, though this didn't make it less of a burden for Father.

They walked in silence. The waves meeting the shore made the only noise between them. Theo surmised the cold was catching up with Tom, who said nothing of the kind but started to take smaller, stiffer steps. Surreptitiously, he kept pace with him and made certain his body was close enough that Tom could lean on him should he stumble.

"I don't know if I should say thank you," Tom said.

Theo chuckled. "You don't have to." He chanced

looking at his reluctant companion. "I certainly didn't think it through, but I know I didn't do it to receive thanks." Of that, at least, he was sure.

"No, I don't think you did."

"I don't know why I. . ."

"Violated my autonomy?" But Tom was almost smiling and it was not an unkind expression. They neared one of the small inns with a dog-shaped wooden sign proclaiming it The Shuck. Theo estimated it had been built last century, and it looked well-kept enough. Although Tom still shivered, he nodded to it. "My uncle keeps this place. It was a public house with a few rooms, first. Ah. . . ages ago. The fashionable thing now is to say it is a hotel, but it truly is still just a pub with a fair number of rooms. An inn. Presently, a boarding house for some old ex-soldiers and one of the town drunks."

"In addition to you, you mean?"

"Yes. A worse one than me, even." Tom grinned. Theo noted how this full smile of his felt more disused than his other expressions. "We can go there. He won't be awake."

"*We?*" Theo echoed Tom, now.

"Unless, of course, you have elsewhere to go. I hope it is not far. I don't think you'd make it."

Theo took a breath and let the cold ground him in his realities. "I do. Less than a mile. I should take my chances going back, even if I'll be cold." At least he didn't need to worry quite so much about being chilled.

"Then I do not wish to impose. I'm sure Mrs. Lloyd will be roused by my arrival. She always sleeps lightly," said Tom. Theo did not know who she was but could guess she was a housekeeper or clerk. "There shall be no way of concealing from her what I have attempted. At the least, she may guess. No matter how strong her suspicions, she will say nothing to anyone who matters." Tom scrubbed a hand over his face. "She would be thrilled to pour you two or three fingers and fuss over you as your coat dries, though."

All of that sounded heavenly, apart from the implication that Tom had succumbed to this melancholy before and someone close to him knew enough about it to be suspicious.

Quietly, Theo said, refusing to remind himself of why he did have to go home, "I shouldn't delay more than I have." He might have been mistaken, but soft disappointment washed over Tom's face, visible in the faint light shed by some of the inn's curtained windows.

He had been right, though, in his assumptions about Tom's coloring. Hazel eyes. Messy dark hair that might be curly. Hard to tell while it was wet. *Forest colors, indeed.*

"Very well," Tom said. When he reached the door, he took a key from an obscured pocket and tried to fit it to the lock with a shaking hand. Theo, who was only slightly less impacted, reached out and helped him keep steady. "Thank you." The lock gave way.

"And all manner of things shall be exceeding well," said Theo, following Mother Julian's quotation with a closed-lipped smile. It was time to return to David, so he couldn't say if the words of reassurance were for him or the man he'd just rescued from drowning.

6

True to her character, Mrs. Lloyd fussed over Tom when she saw how he dripped on the rugs. She was easier to rouse at night than a restless child and he didn't bother to try assuaging her with an innocent explanation. She had been privy to enough of his darker moments, though none so stark as this, that he suspected she knew exactly or roughly what he'd done.

He was far too experienced around the water to have been innocently felled by a rogue wave while standing on the shore.

"If you could fix a cup of tea, Mrs. Lloyd, that would be wonderful." He walked through the entry and barely glanced at her stricken face, squishing his way to the stairs that led to the upper floors.

Her own room was on the ground floor near the kitchen in a converted old storeroom that was quite cozy. While she had not always resided with them, once she was widowed, she had no other family and a landlord who did not wish to let to her without a man in the house. Paul, though he could be a bastard in other ways, would not deny plucky, loyal, efficient Mrs. Lloyd a home.

"What's happened? Do you require a doctor?"

"No. God, no. All's well that ends well." Tom did not want to talk about it. He hardly knew what to say and it wasn't his proclivity for either melancholy or men that posed the problem. He knew she understood the prior and at least suspected the latter. It was Theo, the enigmatic stranger from the beach, who'd captured his thoughts and made it impossible to speak. Nothing and no one else.

Had Tom not given him his medal, it might follow that he was a hallucination. *Or a siren?* If such things as sirens existed. It seemed most plausible here in the warm pub he'd known all his life that Theo was not real at all and somehow he, Mr. Silence Apollyon, had both entered the stunningly cold surf *and* managed to extricate himself from it. *God knows you are lonely enough to have imagined a friend rescuing you from the water.*

"You're tinged with blue." Mrs. Lloyd came closer, keeping her voice down.

About to mount the steps, he stopped.

It had been too dark to see his reflection in a window outside and he had not bothered to glance in the battered gilded mirror on the wall. When he had fished instead of kept an inn, he imagined he was tinged with blue whenever it was cold and windy and damp. But not everyone was used to seeing others in that condition, and certainly, the woman he'd known since he was barely twelve had never seen him look so ragged.

He'd taken some time to grow accustomed to it; initially, it had been unsettling to see men walking about looking like the newly dead if the weather was bad enough.

His fingertips ached as much as his chest burned,

and his arm now felt even more like it had been bent
asunder and shoved back into place at the shoulder.
Theo was not the largest man, and in fact he looked
too svelte to have done what he'd just done, but it belied an evident strength. Tom shivered and it had little
to do with being cold.

"Tea?" He asked, raising his eyebrows, hoping he
did not sound terribly plaintive.

His mind was racing more than his heart, jumping
from image to sensation and skipping from memory to
fantasy. He remembered slipping under the water.
Then very warm, firm lips on his own. He was mired
with regret that he had not succeeded and relief that
he had survived. If there was some kind of divine cre-
ator, they must have been having a lark right now, for
his rescuer seemed opportune and all too perfect.

Even Theo's mode of rescue was unusual in its approach and efficacy. Mouth on mouth. Tom had
known a few others who managed it and believed it
was effective, and all of them worked or lived near water. There were others, such as some doctors or sur-
geons, who espoused it. But in his experience, it meant
someone had knowledge of boats, tides, swimming,
the sea and its moods.

A question in her expression, she shook her head,
then seemed to let the question die and said, "Very
well."

Relieved, he began to go up the stairs. "Thank
you," he said as he went.

His small room was warm thanks to the sleeping
coals in the hearth and tidy thanks to Mrs. Lloyd. It
was the most modest of the rooms they had on offer
and had been his since Paul had taken him as a business partner. Neither of them could abide living with
the other and Tom had no desire to live in the propri-

etor's flat anyway. It was just a mausoleum for a past life. He wrinkled his nose in disgust. Given what he'd discussed just that morning with Mrs. Lloyd, he liked that idea even less.

Poor Paul.

While he would not admit it under duress, he considered himself a spitefully gentle person. He was quite taken with all the fairy stories ending with found love. No one would have expected it from him, for he was not an especially refined man in appearance or mannerisms. Compact but muscular from years of physical labor, his dark hair was always too unruly to ever be slicked into an acceptable style. He had given up. The same years of labor that molded his frame meant he'd been exposed to the elements, giving him more lines than his years might have merited.

Recalling what Theo had said about wet shoes, he removed them first and let them sit close, but not too close, to the fireside. Carefully, he roused the embers into proper flame, then proceeded to undress himself, wincing at how the winter clothes clung, tacky, to his skin. It took longer than usual to shed his layers, all of which he draped over the hearth screen. Satisfied they'd dry and there would probably be no intense damage, he put on a clean pair of drawers.

Rather than risk Mrs. Lloyd's shock should she see him shirtless—she wouldn't mind his undress, but he could hazard a guess he was bruised by rocks and the water itself—he donned a paisley banyan his mother brought him last Christmas. He never wore it, for the saturated ochre colors felt too dandified for his tastes. They suited someone like Theo much better. The ochre would bring out the brown of his eyes, which

Tom had noted in the curtained taproom's barest light before he'd gone inside.

You should not have noticed his eyes at all. Unless he missed his guess, Theo was the sort of man who was generally spoken for.

Anyway, it was not his intention to lose his head in what could be. What already was occupied him enough.

7

As Theo knew it would be, the stately, costly house was silent and dark when he let himself in the unobtrusive servants' entrance. It was only a small house by wealthy standards and he had done this a number of times without rousing any alarm, despite there being one footman called Musgrave who, because of his past military service, was infamous for shooting at anything that moved in the dark.

He was apparently very shaken and prone to nervousness. Ellie, the cook, was protective of him even though he'd once shattered Mrs. Mills' best serving platter.

It possibly said poor things about the present treatment of the Mills' staff that one could enter the house so unnoticed. The only person of their number who cared much about David or his property was Musgrave. In the end, Theo was inclined to side with the ones who didn't care rather than the Mills he had met. All two of them. He'd term David's treatment of the small number of staff as benignly negligent, though.

To be fair, he still seemed rather unused to being

in charge of them and was not especially arrogant, so it came off as aloofness.

His father, on the other hand, had reputedly been quite authoritarian before his health declined. That followed from what Theo knew of him, even if it did not match the idle, confused old man he'd met.

Theo bent to pet the fluffy mouser who crossed his path. She was a silly, loveable thing who was better at receiving affection than catching mice. Ellie called her Mary because no one had volunteered something more fitting for a feline. "At least you don't mind what hour I'm dawdling around at," he said, no louder than a soft breath.

The trick would be convincing David that his walk had been one of the normal, if late, variety. He never came back soaked because he never let himself have a swim. These walks weren't normally so eventful, but he did usually take them, especially when he and David ventured to the coast. He just blamed it on an inherited inability to sleep, which David seemed to accept and wasn't entirely a lie. In truth, it was hard to ignore the water's pull and when he was so close to it, he could not sleep soundly.

It didn't bother him, exactly, but it did create a unique agitation. The higher echelons of society this century tended not to keep early hours, anyway, which afforded him some room to rest as he needed to and have it go unquestioned. Even when he and David kept business hours, it never proved a problem.

He strode lightly through the kitchen, taking care not to jostle any pans or implements that had been left in preparation for the next morning, which by the minute lightening of the sky could not be more than an hour or two away from the present. He was trying to determine the best explanation for his cold, wet clothes when a hand crept out of the corridor's dark and sealed his mouth.

"Your hair is wet."

Theo smiled against the warm palm but said nothing.

David said, quizzically, "All of you is wet. I expected cold, but not wet. And where on earth is your hat?" He dropped his hand after a moment, but not before giving Theo's skin a light stroke with his fingertips.

"Ventured too close to the surf, this time," said Theo. That, like claiming an issue with sleeping, was not strictly an untruth. Theo was an expert in supplying untruths and things that could never be considered lies. Still, to him, it felt like lying. "Did you wait up for me?"

He nodded and Theo saw his straight, white teeth shine in the darkness, catching what little light there was as he smiled. "It is our first holiday alone, so of course I did."

Previously, their holidays had felt more like covert missions involving subterfuge and prevaricating. David's father was happy to allow his son's friend to accompany them or visit them, but of course it was within the parameters of what he deemed an appropriate friendship.

Theo never bothered to explain to Mr. Mills, senior, that such parameters expanded greatly in the halls of Eton and Cambridge to allow for a more generous interpretation of friendship. His pragmatic world had not blended with the worlds of higher learning; David's father never attended university himself.

Regardless, until David inherited everything, their association had been a gauntlet in which they evaded

Mr. Mills and nearly everyone else associated with his household, even though the latter must have been more aware than their employer of the true goings-on. Theo knew servants always were aware of nearly everything.

He watched David with some anticipation. "Very kind of you." He was faintly disconcerted by the way his anticipation attached itself not to the man in front of him and their promised pleasure that his body knew, but to the one he'd just fished out of the treacherous water, who seemed internally lost.

"We shall have to get you out of those clothes."

"I am sorry about the hat," said Theo.

"No matter. You shall have another," David said.

When David kissed him rather boldly, Theo thought, even though the house was asleep and it was unlikely anyone would come upon them, all he could feel was Tom's cold lips and the way they'd shifted to life under his. He sighed and pushed David away, but only just and only gently. "Get me out of these and into something dry and warm, and I shall be forever in your debt," he said, hoping there was a glint in his eye to match his playful speech. "Or tuck me back into bed naked. Your choice."

It seemed to motivate David and distract him from kissing, at least, for he took a step back and said, "Silly of me. Of course." He motioned the way to the narrow, steep servants' stairs that really could have posed a hazard to anyone who wasn't careful.

Theo went, idly touching the St. Julian that fell at the hollow of his collarbones. He'd never intended to complicate his life by doing a good deed, but he was too old to blithely assume he hadn't complicated something. Instinct told him he should take the medal off before David saw it. Why, he could not guess, but he'd learned to trust it when his mind told him something unbidden.

THIS TIME, Theo had come here to leave with the sea's help. It was hard to admit and consider when he rested in a bed that cost more than many men's yearly wages because it made him feel ungrateful. But leaving was his original plan. He wanted love if he was going to risk divulging the most important parts of himself to another, and he'd been leaning into complacency for months. The guard he kept around his identity was a learned behavior, one he knew from his father, and he could not disregard it for David. This reticence told him he did not want to stay.

To leave in the best way he knew, he needed the sea and there was no better opportunity than David's yearly sojourn to the coast. He glanced at the body next to him. David wasn't cruel or crude. There just wasn't any magic to their association and when the association itself was patently illegal if not derided, Theo could not see the logic in attempting to settle.

But because he couldn't, he felt churlish. *You're fed, you're clothed, you don't truly need to work,* he thought, trying to make himself see sense. He wasn't deeply unhappy or at all mistreated, and he could admit thousands were in much worse straits.

Nonetheless, a well-rooted yearning told him this was not all, this was not right, and this was not for him. He'd have to find some way to articulate it to David, who despite all his bluster was deeply uncertain of his place in the world, and he'd try to do so gently and without any mention of the preternatural. It wasn't David's fault, after all, and Theo wasn't certain his beliefs could be expanded.

The sun slipped through a small gap in the curtains and its light would have tickled David's nose if it were a feather. Theo chuckled to himself. Unless he put his mind to rising, David slept through anything. Sitting up, he decided he would visit one of the several tea stalls nearby. Night wasn't the only time he took walks, and if he *happened* to come across a certain melancholic innkeeper who abused the bottle, then no one would think anything of it. While it was a Mills family tradition to come after Christmas to Cromer, the number of staff in the house was still minimal and they were on good terms with him.

He managed to dress and get out without crossing anyone's path.

He still cursed himself for being eager, but could not seem to help it.

8

The sun blazed. Had it been summer, it would be quite warm, but as it was, the light seemed to turn everything to cold glass. He pulled down the brim of his second-best hat and changed direction mid-stride. It really wasn't a tea stall he wanted or sought.

"I'm sure The Shuck has tea," he mumbled. And Tom had mentioned it was presently more of a boardinghouse, less of an inn or a pub, which signified a certain coziness that to his mind meant tea and a hearth.

He told himself he wanted to see how Tom fared, but in actuality, he just wanted to *see* him.

An older man was behind the small reception desk in the common room that served as an entryway, and one glance told Theo he was probably not supposed to be there. His attire looked like a ragpicker's and he listed to the side like a dubiously functional chimney. As Theo approached, the distinct waft of gin surfaced in his nose.

"Good morning," said the dubiously functional chimney man.

"Is it still morning?" Theo said. He smiled.

The man did not. "The sun is up, sir, the sun is *up*."

"Well, that is a prerequisite for morning. Or, at least, any stretch of morning past dawn."

His words seemed to stun the man, who blinked and gazed at him as though he was the most brilliant of scholars about to deliver a fantastic speech on the scientific qualities of light or sound. "Quite so, sir, quite so indeed."

While Theo could have continued on in this vein for hours as he was deeply tickled, he was still relieved —thrilled—when Tom's voice carried between them. "Benson, that is a splendid job you've done."

Benson drew himself up to a slightly less precarious angle and sat up straight in the chair he used as a perch. "No need to patronize me, Mr. Apollyon. I helped your uncle with this place, once upon a time. In fact, I helped implement this desk. We had to rebuild it when Sommers dropped it from the back of his cart. A careless fellow, if I do say so, but then I personally would never trust a man from Manchester."

"What's wrong with anyone from Manchester?" asked Theo.

Benson physically recoiled as though to wind himself up to make a reply, then expelled a large sigh. "Never you mind. Keep to pronouncements about the sun."

And judging by his age, Theo felt the era in which Benson could have really supplied help to anybody would have been during Wellington's prime. But he kept the quip to himself. He also couldn't picture a marked reception area, no matter how small, being in a pub or inn like this when it was first built. But times changed and with those changes came new ideas of class, of standing, of what one was owed in service or deference. It must have been a gesture to appeal to more genteel patrons, some of whom would not want to settle their accounts or ask for directions or where to dine in a taproom.

"I wasn't patronizing you at all," said Tom, and as he came around Theo to approach Benson in all of his belligerence, Theo tried diligently to maintain his politely cheerful expression. Laughter would not do. "I just like to give praise where it is due."

Benson's scowl lessened and he switched his attention to inspect Theo. Coming off his perch with a noise not unlike the fall of a horse's hooves on the aged wood floor, he walked toward Theo with an appraising gleam in his watery eyes. "This one is well shifty." Theo remained still. "Be sure to watch him, Mr. Apollyon. He might make his way out with the silver."

Theo did not contradict him, for he had a personal rule not to argue with the elderly. He also could not deny that he was shifty in the most obvious sense of the term. But the closer Benson crept, the more Theo had the sense he was playacting and this apparently shaky grasp on reality was a sham. It interested him, for he could not say why an old man would pretend to have tenuous sanity.

Tom put a hand on Benson's shoulder. "I will watch him."

I wish you would, thought Theo.

"You have my word. Now, do run along." Tom spoke as though he addressed an older relative, but one of which he was very fond. This made Theo smile, which he promptly hid with his hand. Someway, he inferred Benson would be quick to glass him for a perceived slight. Where a glass was, he had no idea, for the immediate vicinity seemed free of glassware. But it was possible Benson had something dangerous hidden on his person in those smelly, voluminous layers.

"I'd wanted to find some tea, yes," said Benson, in the day's apparent excuse for going anywhere. And that was that. Benson stopped inspecting Theo and scampered through a doorway that led a few steps lower than the present level.

"My apologies," said Tom. "He really is harmless, just a little addled."

"And fond of gin. Hello, Mr. Drunkard."

It might have been his eyes seeing a reaction they wanted to see, but Tom appeared to blush slightly. He said, "Well, addled, before that. But yes. He loves gin. His right leg pains him, he says, and he maintains the drink is medicinal only." Tom peered over the desk Benson had been supposed to man, apparently satisfied all of the ledgers were still intact. "He's been lingering downstairs lately, convinced Yule brought more witches in from Norwich. I said there were probably witches here to begin with. He told me I was right, but that the ones from Norwich were worse than the ones already here."

It was hard not to stare at Tom in the glorious daylight, so Theo had to pace his staring or he would risk looking addled, as well. "How lurid."

"Quite. He also says he is descended from witchhunters, which could be true."

Theo did not want to point out that although he had never met a witch resembling the demonic type, plenty of people existed who could not be explained with rational means. *Yet.* He felt philosophy and biology could eventually expand to explain selkies and probably an entire host of other creatures once said to be impossible. For all he knew, learned men in secret laboratories were making headway on such an endeavor. He certainly hoped not, but ordinary people were imprisoned for supposed madness all the time, so it stood to reason there could be more clandestine facilities.

He cleared his mind of such dark thoughts. "He looks like one, or what I'd picture one to be like. You know, my employer's family supposedly had a witch-hunting branch, but the fact of the matter is, I cannot picture it."

"Mr. Mills is your employer, correct?"

"Yes, I've been his secretary for a good two years, now. Over two years, actually."

Employer was a very mild word for what he and David got up to, but it was the most innocuous, and David's father *had* once remarked that their descendent had been a witch-hunter in the vein of the greats. Theo, knowing what was good for him, had not bothered to point out how disgusting the practice was. Mr. Mills had been of a religious bent, and more than religious, he was zealous, which made him fairly unpleasant.

Theo tried to imagine David doing anything that involved the arcane arts—if one were to believe in them, which Theo did—or fraud and hostility, which was more often the case in histories of witches and their hunters. While prim and prone to self-righteousness, David probably lacked the steel required to have zealous beliefs.

It was also supremely difficult to think any man who adored his latest suit and shoes or a good punt on the River Cam to the amount David did would manage any of the adventurous things required to hunt preternatural beings.

Or the terrible ones involved in scapegoating accused witches, thought Theo.

No, torture did not seem like it could be David's raison d'être. Neither had it seemed like his father's. In all, if the Mills had come from militant stock, it was now a defanged and rather comfortable bloodline whose men were fond of exquisitely woven cloth and cigarettes.

"Yes, David's—ah, Mr. Mills'—father said they were descended from a man who looked up to Matthew Hopkins," Tom said. He frowned and added, "We didn't remain friendly, but his family's history, such as it might be, had little to do with that."

Sensing more to the assertion, Theo sought to change the topic. Everyone did seem to be aware of everyone else's business in this place, so it wouldn't surprise him if David and Tom had been anything at all. The finer nuances of friendly seemed clear to him, and so did calling someone by their given name. Those nuances might not be clear if he wasn't accustomed to seeking meaning where others needed only the most obvious one.

Though they were of different habits and likely had been since childhood, Theo conjectured that David would have found Tom very tantalizing. Part of the allure, Theo knew from observation and experiencing others' perceptions of his own status in society, was that very difference. He'd been a bit of rough before and supposed Tom had, too.

After a smile, Theo said, "But your Benson does not seem threatening. Not really. If he is a zealot, he appears to be on your good side."

Tom chuckled. "Everyone around here does know him, but I think he would frighten any visitors. I wouldn't have left him alone, but Mrs. Lloyd needed some help moving a crate into the kitchen."

It was little better to think of Tom moving a crate

than it was to stare at him without cause. He was strong and lithe. Theo said, with his eyes momentarily on Tom's chest as he contemplated what it might look like under his shirt and coat, "How is your arm, then?"

"Painful, but I'll live." The barest of smiles surfaced on his face.

"That is good of you to help her."

They must not have as many employees this time of year, Theo reasoned.

Tom seemed to read his mind. "It's a little leaner right now. We aren't keeping as much help."

"Well, I shall let you know if I am ever in need of a decent position. You seem like you'd supply a good one." Even to Theo's own mind, which was usually of a slightly devilish turn, it sounded a bit crude when he hadn't meant it to be. He cleared his throat. "And if I ever wish to move away from the city to reside on the coast."

There was the small detail of how he lived with David in a lovely house with a wonderful view of Chapelfield Gardens, but if he'd been planning on running away, already, he could do it this way. *You cannot run away simply to run to someone else,* he told himself, trying to be firm about it. A creature like him was supposed to attract men, but not keep attaching itself to them. Such a pattern, he knew, might lead to nothing but trouble. David wasn't the specific reason for his fear, and although his father had made it obvious why such a thing was to be avoided—any person who had his skin could keep him captive—it was just a base, uncontrolled instinct to be terrified by the notion.

In the best case, he would experience that most elusive of things: love.

The worst does not bear contemplating. Visions,

thoughts of his skin being separated from him, or of torture for his differences, momentarily occupied his mind. He was no witch or seer, but his kind had often found themselves treated the same according to their own whispers and rumors. Never mind the skin-stealing. They were often treated with hostility and distrust.

He still felt more for all of the innocents, especially women, whose mundane differences or choices marked them as deviant. On the surface, he was nothing but a mild-mannered man with good taste, a knack for organization, and an accent that never belied where he was born and had grown up. He could talk himself out of almost any trouble and be given the benefit of the doubt.

Much to his surprise, Tom tilted his head and said one word. "Do."

Pleased, he nodded. "I've done many things, but most recently retrained to be an impeccable book-keeper and secretary. Obviously. Right at the moment, though..." he shrugged. "I am not here for business. I wanted to see how you were getting on."

He watched Tom swallow. Perhaps he was thinking over how to reply. Theo noted more about his person, comfortable in the pause. His clothes were simple and in good condition and he clearly took good care of them even if he did not seem to mind whether he was particularly in fashion.

Again Theo thought of the woods, of shadows cast by leaves and under ferns.

"I'm well enough."

But for the quiet note of shame in his voice, Theo might have believed him. "Would you like to. . . step out?"

Tom shook his head. "I should stay here. My uncle

is still indisposed, and it isn't Mrs. Lloyd's task to mind things."

"You mind the taproom, too?"

"When it is not empty."

"Does it not. . ."

As wry as he was perceptive, Tom said, "Tempt me? No. My intemperance isn't so foolhardy." He lifted a pen from his coat pocket, as though to show off a new purchase. "If it's an inky day, one when I find myself subjected to a black mood, I'm far more likely to imbibe too much."

Charmed, Theo felt he understood. "And today is not inky?"

"Today is. . ." Tom paused as he replaced the pen. "Not inky. No." He glanced up at Theo. "Yesterday was. I was drowning in ink."

And so you tried to drown in truth.

Before Theo could make a reply that would not betray Tom's confidence but might indicate he inferred the connection, Tom said, "Come. We can speak more freely in the taproom. I will be able to hear anyone who ventures inside for lodging, as unlikely as it is."

While he knew he might not have time for a pint, he wished to have one. He could make his excuses to David and no harm would result.

Besides, Theo would accept no reason why he should not be free to converse with a new acquaintance. Briefly stymied, he was considering almost every choice in his personal life he had made to date when Tom said, "All right?"

"Pardon?"

"You looked as though you wanted to say something."

"Did I?" There was so much he wished to say

lodged in his throat and he did not know how to say any of it.

Tom took the few steps down into the taproom and widened its curtains to capture more of the sun-light. "Indeed."

"I do suppose I have a lot to say, but it is truly of no matter." He removed his hat and placed it upon the bar, sitting on one of the tall chairs with a low back, content to watch as Tom poured him a dram of what looked and smelled like whisky. "Tell me why today isn't death by ink."

Tom slid the small glass toward him. He took his time to say one word, muscles shifting in his jaw as he was quiet.

Then he said, "You."

Me?

9

Immediately as he said it, Tom flushed.

It was like being possessed; he hadn't meant to utter, "You." Yet, he had.

But he did not rush to take it back and kept outwardly calm, or so he thought, and watched Theo's reaction to such an audacious and succinct reply. He didn't need to watch so much as feel. The same sense of knowing that existed the night before was still strong, and Tom was not about to admit he'd known Theo was inside the inn before he'd seen or heard him.

"Mind that wet patch on the floor," Mrs. Lloyd had said as he'd jostled the crate into place and hefted it inside, and he'd needed her warning because he'd been distracted by the sudden warm, almost pins-and-needles, bubbles on the breeze feeling that seemed to signify Theo's near proximity.

He'd foolishly turned his head to look for him in the kitchen, but he was not there, of course.

"What is it?" Mrs. Lloyd asked.

"Nothing at all." Even though it was something. Poor Theo had been cornered by rheumatic, boisterous Benson. He was one of their older residents who hailed from Norwich, had one younger brother whom he called Timmy—even though Timmy greatly preferred to be known as Timothy—drank far too much, and claimed he could speak to the dead, or identify a witch on sight.

This was all tolerated because he was an old friend of Paul's.

Since he did seem to speak to people who were not there and the Apollyon family had its stories about witches, Tom did not know what to believe and kept an open mind. It seemed too outlandish to think every elderly person who spoke to nothing was communing with spirits, but it wouldn't matter to him if Benson was.

He was an amiable fellow if left to keep his own beliefs and habits. They'd made several trips to Norwich together because Tom found his company implausibly uplifting and not troubling in the least.

Tom tilted the bottle and poured himself a small amount of whisky. It couldn't hurt. He glanced at Theo, almost daring him to say something.

Catching his eye, Theo said, "You'll find no censure from me." He crumpled his brown hair with his free hand. It was mussed already, not curly, but clearly unruly when left to its own devices.

"Good. I don't take well to it."

The understatement was comical. In actuality, if someone told him not to do something, he was more likely to do it, and if he was told to do something—unless it was patently related to business or safety—he rarely did it promptly. He supposed the tendency had mellowed a little, but it was no longer good-natured and experimental as it had been when he was a child.

Now, he knew he could be called sour. He had been. *Or a bastard.* He smirked at the thought.

"Hm?"

"Nothing. I was only thinking of what a curmudgeon I am." Before he could remind himself to drink slowly because it was actually a delicious thing, he took all the whisky into his mouth and swallowed without a wince.

"I don't know if I'd agree," said Theo. The only indication of his surprise was his slightly raised eyebrows. In daylight, his eyes were close to the color of his scarf, a shade close to a strong cup of black tea in sunlight.

Tom set his glass down and almost poured himself another finger or two, but refrained. He changed the subject. "You must be an excellent swimmer."

"I am." Theo straightened in his seat and grinned. "Thank you for noticing."

"Swam in shoes, a coat. . ."

"I've had immense amounts of practice."

"Not around here."

"Pardon?" said Theo.

Tom smiled, thinking he'd gleaned something personal Theo would rather downplay, and leaned on his forearms, resting them on the bar. "I suppose you sound American. Well, almost every fifth or sixth word does. So. . . perhaps not American. But it's a very gentle accent, whatever it is."

"I'm not from the states. And I've lived here—England—for a while. But I'm not from here, either."

"That's nothing to be ashamed of." Nothing so wonderful came from being English, in his experience, and Tom had worked with a handful of men from the states, most of whom came from New York or Maine.

He actually found he got on better with them than his countrymen, not that one should really make assumptions about an entire country after meeting a handful of its citizens. Teasing, he added, "I won't tell anyone."

"Thank you. It's my most shameful secret," said Theo. A disquiet lurked in his eyes, Tom thought, even though he spoke in jest. "How much I've moved around."

"I would never break your—"

"Oh, my," said Mrs. Lloyd from the doorway adjacent to the entryway and common room. "I'd no idea you had company!" Tom shifted to look at her, tearing his attention away from Theo. She stared at the two of them as though she had forgotten Tom was capable of forming acquaintances.

It was hard to say, but he thought she was pleased by another person's presence near him.

"Shall I bring biscuits?"

"No, Mrs. Lloyd."

"Sandwiches?"

"I don't think we require any," Tom said.

"But it is well past breakfast."

"So I see," said Tom, eyeing the clock on the wall, set just above her head.

"Are you not hungry?"

"No," said Tom.

"It isn't right to entertain without something to nibble."

"I'm not entertaining!"

But she scurried away, presumably to reappear shortly with a plate of cold meats or biscuits. He hoped it was not sandwiches. He rarely cared for them. There was, likewise, no point in calling after her to say he was not *entertaining*. He didn't think one could entertain one's rescuer, particularly when one had been rescued from attempted self-harm. It had to complicate things, for it was not as though they'd met while visiting the same tailor.

What a lovely world it would be if we'd crossed paths under better circumstances. Now that the shock had ebbed with the foul frame of mind, he was finding he was rather embarrassed by succumbing to the waves of ink. He disparaged Paul for much the same thing, and this realization made him both tense and terse.

"She is a silly creature," Tom said.

Theo bit his lip, just, then said, "She means well, I am sure."

It had been years since Mrs. Lloyd had seen him conversing so amicably with anyone, so Tom could see why she was adamant that someone who seemed to be having a decent conversation with him should be met with *something to nibble.* She was like a second mother, or perhaps a grandmother or older aunt, and Tom could not fault her.

"She does look after me as best she can." He placed his glass to the side at last and smiled dolefully at Theo. "You see, I am given to being rather taciturn."

"But you keep an inn."

Chuckling, Tom said, "Yes, I know. I. . . my mother asked me to return here and help my uncle. He's my father's brother, and she didn't think it was right to leave him alone, as he's. . ." despite feeling comfortable enough to divulge the circumstances, there was a small chance Paul could venture downstairs. He had become quite the recluse in recent days, but he did own the inn and might wander at will. "Struggling to manage."

"You seem personable to me."

"I can perform with patrons. It's all an act." He shrugged. "I'm fortunate enough to look trustworthy, too. I'm not sure what that means, exactly, but I favor my uncle and my father, and people seem to trust them. Well, him. My father isn't with us."

"And I am a patron."

After a pause, Tom said, "No. No, I'm. . . I like talking to you."

Theo dimpled but said nothing.

I have to look away from that expression or I'll go mad, Tom thought. He said, "But... when we have them. That's spring and summer, largely, and a fair few in autumn. Paul—my uncle—noted he usually has more in the winter than there are now, too, but some years are slower. When they're around, it's. . . I slip into it. All the niceties, the genteel deference." He tongued his lower lip, thinking. "I wear smarter clothes, too. Have them laundered more often."

Had Tom stayed local, he knew he would have had a better rapport with the regulars. He'd only worked at The Shuck during summers and some holidays. Instead, he drifted until Mother had a fateful conversation with Paul about the state of The Shuck's future. He didn't know the particulars, really, but having no children of his own, Paul conceded it would be wise to have Tom year-round. When the time came, it would be easier for them to transition from one publican or proprietor to another and The Shuck would be kept in the family.

There were two pitfalls to this plan: first, like Paul and for the same reasons as his own, Tom had no children. Second, he had never stayed in one place for long as a grown man. It was not the sea he disliked; in fact, given his choice, he would have stayed in a hut near the waves, speaking to no one. *Repairing nets or boats,* he thought.

Theo peered at him, but it was difficult to divine

what he was thinking. Without having his peripheral sense of Theo's presence, Tom would have assumed he'd put him off. But because Theo's ambient effervescence hadn't abated, he assumed Theo was merely deciding what polite thing to say next.

Surely, unlike Tom was every other moment, he was not thinking of the feel of their bodies together or the press of warm lips upon a cold mouth—

"I know."

"I'm sorry?" It was ridiculous to feel so, but he hoped, then dreaded, Theo had managed to peer inside his mind. He cleared his throat.

"I understand the things we do to survive. Well, that's a dramatic way of saying it. But, I mean, to work. I understand having to work or change one's profession." Theo finished his whisky. "That was delicious, by the way."

"It's from one of the islands."

"I've visited several."

"Always wanted to." A ridiculous glimmer of a nonexistent future came, then—he and Theo could have a wonderful time traveling. Tom nodded to the empty glass, shaking his head a little to clear it. That was a ludicrous thing to think. "Another?"

"Best not. I slipped out to check on you, and it wouldn't do to return intoxicated." Theo's grin was a hair lopsided, and it cracked Tom's heart.

You came to check on me? "Right. . . you. . ." Since it was the middle of the working day, Tom said, "Bookkeeping. You'll have to return to work."

"No. Well, yes. But there's something of a Christmas lull. Hogmanay lull. I left the house without anyone being the wiser and came here."

Hogmanay? That could indicate where he grew up, certainly.

Mrs. Lloyd returned with a platter of the most mis-matched but endearing nibbles. Tom spied sand-wiches, several kinds of biscuits, cheeses, and dried fruits. "Really, Mrs. Lloyd?"

"You've been eating like a bird of late," she said. She wasn't wrong, although he wasn't aware anyone had noticed. With Mother remarried and living in Norwich as she always had, Mrs. Lloyd was perhaps the only person who would see him often enough to understand his habits.

He snorted. "But who else have you invited? This is enough for five men and I haven't the right hat for the occasion." With a dramatic look at his shirt, then coat, he said, "Clearly not the right colors for the season, either."

Theo beamed as Mrs. Lloyd set the tray upon the bar between them. She blushed, but kept her hands steady. While she was many things, easily flustered was not one, so Tom noted the stain in her cheeks with amused interest. Once a renowned—if that was the correct term to apply; he didn't know what she preferred—local courtesan, she was not easily swayed by a sunny smile or a handsome man.

Well, it seemed Theo had that arresting effect upon both of them, then.

"I might have shown too much enthusiasm," she said. "But this way, you shall have your pick of what you'd like and you won't starve. You know I am not against drinking spirits, but I tend to believe one should eat solids alongside them." Her eyes were bright behind her spectacles. "Gentlemen." With a nod and the barest extra glance at Theo, she quit the room in a wave of skirts and soft rose perfume.

"I like her," said Theo. Without hesitation, he chose what appeared to be a watercress sandwich.

"Do not let her hear you say so."

"Why not?"

"You have her blushing with only a smile. I cannot guess what she would do if you said you liked her, and she's the only one with any sense around here."

Another grin from Theo, and this time it was Tom who blushed. He knew he wasn't pale enough for it to show and he presently hadn't shaved for a week, so his coloring was largely obscured. He took a piece of dried apple and held it, forgetting to put it in his mouth until the door facing the street opened, allowing a bit of cold air inside.

"There must be someone else with sense rattling about this building. Your uncle, maybe?" Theo wasn't grinning, now, but he was smiling. Teasing. It was pleasant.

Tom said, after he finished chewing, "That deeply depends upon the day. He *is* of sound mind, but his life hasn't been the easiest. Sense isn't all he's interested in."

"That must be a family trait, Mr. Apollyon. You do seem to be a rather fanciful lot."

He couldn't immediately place the voice or the person, which wasn't a concern given his occupation. Whether word of mouth or personal knowledge, most of those who entered the premises knew his surname. Tom had also worked hard to guard himself against others' feelings and sensations when they simply just entered The Shuck, for onboarding so many of those was exhausting.

But Theo, even with his back turned, apparently could instantly divine the speaker's identity. All it took to dash his levity was the short, cool sentence. He looked up at Tom with a grimace of apology. Yet it was the finally-diffused effervescence that truly made his

displeasure known. And when Tom looked at the man
who'd just entered his uncle's establishment, he
wished he always allowed others' feelings to precede
them after all. Mr. David Mills stood in the taproom,
looking as out of place as a proverbial bull in the
china shop, his blue eyes striking even from across the
room.

10

D avid eyed Tom and Theo, enjoying how his entrance had caught Theo unawares. His mouth, normally so inviting, gaped as he twisted where he sat to look at David. "Hello, Theo," he said.

He was surprised to see Theo here in the company of a man from whom he was so different. Where Theo was deliberate and chose his words with care, Tom moved through his life as though heedless of the consequences. *I can't even recall what trade he settled on.* It was something to do with fishing or nets. He knew he'd worked on the docks for some time, as well.

The prolific local tongues said he'd returned to care for his ailing uncle, assuming responsibilities at one of the family's two pubs. The latter appeared true, but with no need or inclination to visit the establishment, David had not seen the elder Mr. Apollyon in months. Years, more accurately, and not only because he'd avoided the place after being told off by his father for carrying on with Tom. Even if he had gone in for a pint, he might not have seen its proprietor, depending on what time of year it was.

Most other people observed the new year when it came, but Mr. Apollyon let it slip by.

If he'd been pining for someone that long, he wouldn't have the vigor to show his face either, and everyone speculated his man Alistair had not been just his employee.

On that, he and Mr. Apollyon could commiserate.

"David," said Tom. True to his memories of a younger Tom, this one seemed disdainful, even petulant. From David's perspective, he couldn't see how Tom *wouldn't* be irked at the state of his own life.

"If it's a room you're in need of, we have a large selection," said Tom, his knuckles a little pale as he clutched the bar's edge like he was bracing for a storm, "it being the low season. That is, if your dear father has turned you out, again, to. . . ah. . . learn you a lesson."

The jibe was purposeful and David almost admired its precision. He and Tom had, on more than one memorable occasion, made good use of the rooms upstairs. Their temperaments weren't very compatible, though at one time, he did wish something else could have bloomed. Impossible as it was to hope for something of the kind.

In fact, the last time he'd been inside The Shuck, he'd told Tom he wished it was cursed. He'd felt trapped, and disdainful, and embarrassed that his father had caught them in flagrante delicto, and sorely regretted that they had been caught. Not that he'd said any of that—more or less, he just said it should be cursed to match its ill-advised name.

As the only son in a family with considerable means and some social connections, Father never wanted to disown him. But he was stringent in his retaliations until old age sapped his energy.

"You know, my father hated it when people would say that. He'd always be sure to tell me it was *teach*, after the fact."

Tom said, "Oh, I can imagine. Still, *if* you need a room. . ."

"That won't be necessary," said David. "I was merely passing by and happened to see my friend, here, in your taproom."

"He is an acquaintance of Mrs. Lloyd's, and she has told everyone who might listen about the shipment we received from Scotland," said Tom.

David hadn't any notion of what the shipment might be within this brazen lie. "Oh?"

"Whisky, of course."

Theo's head tilted toward Tom as he spoke, and David's annoyance flared. He didn't understand how they were acquainted, but he didn't have to enjoy the idea regardless of how they'd met—even, or especially, if he and Tom had what might politely be termed a *history*.

"Naturally."

"Your father would appreciate it. I can have some sent to him."

That was more of Tom's pointed sarcasm: Father had been a rather irksome teetotaler. Mother had been less fervent about it and sometimes took a nip of brandy, but because she had died first, her tempering influence waned by the time David was old enough to experiment with drink. Theo knew all of this, and he wrinkled his nose, no doubt weighing the pros and cons of speaking up.

However Theo had met him, he didn't know Tom well enough to understand he was clever, but the sharp kind of clever that didn't care for niceties.

While David had intended to break with Theo

soon, perhaps after the new year, the merest stray thought of him conducting anything with Tom rankled. He glanced from one man to the other, trying to decide if he was being needlessly suspicious or not.

"Haven't you heard? Father is dead."

It hadn't been an enormous blow to him because he did not think Father was capable of being close to anyone and especially him, although the done thing wouldn't be to admit one's father had been rather cruel in his pursuit of moral and social rigidity.

"I hadn't, no," said Tom. David disliked the sympathy that meandered into his expression. They'd known each other for decades by now, but hadn't had a reason to cross paths as men. The Mills had no need for an inn when they kept a home in Cromer and it was large enough to house several guests. But having grown up seeing David during the summers, Tom was at least somewhat aware of Mr. Mills' predisposition for prickly and restrictive behavior. David had not told him everything.

But he wasn't displaying sympathy for the death; it was sympathy for what David had endured. Despite, David thought, the acrid way they'd parted. A smaller internal voice insisted that some things simply ended and very few people were capable of grace at that age. He couldn't, it whispered, hold Tom to the same standards of anyone with more experience of the heart. Especially not when it had been his father who insisted they break it off.

He disregarded what that little, internal voice had to say, although he knew it was correct. He should hold his father responsible.

"I always forget how. . . heedless of society. . . you are." That much hadn't changed, at least not by his visual assessment of the man before him. Shadows under his eyes, clothes rumpled, wavy hair cropped in deference to expectations while his stubbled face defied them.

"I was on a boat or hauling something around when it happened, most likely. I've only been here from October," said Tom. He didn't rise to David's barb and instead reached for a clean pint glass. David narrowed his eyes in an unspoken question. "I recall you enjoy ale rather than whisky."

He nodded just the once and could not keep the slightest closed-mouth smile from his lips.

"Ale it is, then," Tom said.

Again, Theo's head tilted as though registering a sound only he heard. But he said nothing.

His Theo was a consummate observer of people, that was certain.

Taking a few steps forward, then, David saw the plate sitting between Theo and Tom. "What a wonderful spread. Though, isn't it a little early to be enjoying pints?" He took a chair next to Theo. "And I wasn't aware you knew Mr. Apollyon, Theo, even if you do know the wonderful Mrs. Lloyd." Feeling no need to sham his preferences around Tom, he nudged Theo gently, who smiled with some reserve.

"We came across each other on one of my *very* late-night strolls," Tom said.

"Still can't sleep?" David said to his back.

Tom shrugged as he pulled the pint. "I might sleep better if I could hear the water, but it's too cold now to leave the windows open. I'll survive until spring."

It was difficult for David to access his own interior sentiments and trying to express them seemed to augment the difficulty in accessing them. His mind and mouth felt permanently disconnected. Here were his past and present loves, or if not loves, then comrades in arms, and he could make neither heads nor tails of it. Despite everything that had happened between them, he was *pleased* to see Tom was here and because it was not how he expected to feel it made him surly.

Things could have been so very different had his father not intervened, but then, there was no way to maintain such a friendship forever. He would still have to marry one day. He frowned. Tom's uncle hadn't, and through some kind of strategy, he was free of those conventions.

It certainly felt as though he had to strategize to be as he was. He knew he was fortunate to be affluent because it afforded him privacy and with that came ability. Theo had once remarked he had anonymity without wealth, which suited him, and David could not tell which he'd prefer. It seemed like a pointless exercise to imagine what he wasn't.

All he really understood was Tom made him feel a relentless buzz on his skin, much like what he fancied electricity must feel as it hummed into one's house. Theo produced a similar sensation, but his was warmer and more reminiscent of inhaling from a newly lit cigarette.

"Will you?" Theo said.

Tom glanced at him over his lean shoulder, one eyebrow raised.

Theo clarified, saying, "Survive until spring?" Then his smile was for Tom, as though David weren't there at all.

David stared. He'd never seen that expression on Theo's face. He interjected, "It's possible he won't. The Apollyons not only lack sense, they're also incredibly prone to melancholy."

Sliding the pint glass to David, Tom said, "Some of us truly are. I won't deny it."

"You always did seem to have it worse than your father. And your uncle. Although, I've not seen Mr. Apollyon, senior, for an age." David sipped. "Are you keeping his body in the attic?"

"Wouldn't you like to know?" Since it was uttered with his back turned once again, David imagined the smirk on Tom's lips. "You won't have any heartfelt confessions from me. It's not in my nature to be so emotional."

That wasn't true and they both knew it. He spoke his mind even if he did not speak much of it. With the soft, loaded glances abundant between him and Tom, David would wager Theo somehow knew these aspects of his temperament, too. While he'd started the morning with thoughts of how he and Theo might best end their arrangement, he was now suddenly consumed by the idea of preventing Tom from having something he had once wanted. It was an infantile response, but unfortunately, he didn't know how to combat it.

Sure as the crystalline sunlight flaring into the room with its smoke-stained Georgian crossbeams and full bottles of drink, he saw what Tom possibly didn't, yet— because he was seemingly incapable of believing someone might esteem him, much less love him—Theo was smitten.

So is Tom, David thought.

It rippled tenuously between them, and true, if it had not once been directed toward David to some extent, he might not notice at all. Tom was hard to get to know and he was protean. David once thought this was by design, but had revised his opinion to include the possibility that some people were just born as changeable elderly men. He eyed the pewter threads that were barely visible between Theo and Tom, hanging from Tom's shoulder to Theo's wrist at rest on the bar, and blinked. Then they were gone.

"I know he's still with us," said David, relenting in his macabre joke. "Just last week, I found myself wondering if this period was any easier for him compared to the others that came before."

Theo took a biscuit and nibbled. "My word, everyone does know everyone around here. I don't understand how any of you manage to do anything with all the business you know about your neighbors."

"Spoken like a true American. You all have too much space." But as he said it, David realized he didn't know if Theo was actually from the states.

"I'm not," said Theo, confirming his unspoken question. "I have spent time there, which may account for my *uncouth* tone." Merrily, he added, before crunching the rest of his biscuit, "You've just never asked where I'm from."

"What are you, then?" Tom, as was his custom, had started on another dram of whisky.

"I, my good barkeeper. . . innkeeper. . . publican. . . proprietor. . . hail from Leith," said Theo.

"Leith?" David couldn't help raising his eyebrows. He'd never been north of York. "You don't sound like you come from Lei–"

"Oh, no, I don't. I'm aware of that," said Theo. He patted David's arm. "You're proof I don't sound like it at all. How long have we known each other, and you have never been able to tell? Again, not that you've asked."

Peeved, David said, "Yes. Quite. Apologies, old chap."

Tom, the devil, said, "I enjoy Leith. Been there several times. And now that you've mentioned it, I can hear little tells."

David might have been able to overlook their shared experience he did not know about had Theo not leaned forward slightly, causing a thin, gold chain to slip from his collar as he said, "You're only saying it to make me feel better."

While it could have been any number of chains, David had never seen Theo wear jewelry. He didn't usually favor many accessories, so any new addition was obvious. There was an animal skin he often wore when it was cold, nondescript and gray as soot, which David often had to beg him to exchange for a scarf. It was one of the reasons why he'd assumed Theo came from somewhere in North America. They had all kinds of fur trappers there, he'd thought.

But when the chain came to rest on Theo's collarbone and a small, oval medal pulled it taut, he swallowed. One look at Tom told him the necklace was no longer on its original neck, a neck he'd quite like to throttle at that present instant. The medal was from Tom's maternal grandmother, who enjoyed the words of St. Julian.

He'd never taken it off when they were lads, and it had usually glinted just under shirts, a tiny flash on a person who otherwise wished to attract no attention at all. Yes. David concluded he must know precisely, exactly, entirely what had transpired last night. It felt momentous and he did not want it to be so.

11

C hecking train timetables felt alien because Tom hadn't gone to Norwich for weeks. When he did travel there, now, it was usually to visit his gran's grave or accompany Benson to Timothy's narrow house off Magdalen Street. He wandered as though it kept him alive, like breathing or eating or sleeping, but traveling with purpose didn't feel the same. It didn't always yield good results and often left him more restless than when he started off on the journey.

This was why he had always volunteered to help Benson. If the purpose was directly for someone else, it was usually more pleasant for him. Tom shifted under his bedclothes, rolled to face the dying fire, and set his timetables aside on an adjacent chair. He could decide tomorrow.

Regardless, Paul probably needs to show himself before I venture any more than minutes away from this place.

Gran would remain dead, after all. He needed to visit her more often. Mother would be happy to see him no matter when he arrived on her step. The man who was supposed to be his new father, on the other hand, would be less happy. He rolled his eyes. As though a grown man needed a father at all, but Mother seemed content and unharmed, which mattered.

His own parents had been happy and neither of them was prone to coldness. They were loving, so if he had always been an introspective, disjointed creature prone to mental fragility, it was not their fault.

He certainly felt shattered today.

Probabilities weren't his forte, so he couldn't begin to guess what the odds might be that David would somehow be involved with his jaunty and unlikely savior. Unlikelier, still, that David managed to locate Theo in a place where he hadn't ventured for years. He supposed The Shuck was well-located and anyone on a walk could happen to pass by, yet the timing was comical and David wasn't known to idle around town.

But as Paul might say when he did speak again, there weren't coincidences.

"Dear, I thought you might like some tea." Mrs. Lloyd knocked at his door.

"Do you ever think I would enjoy something stronger?" he mumbled, smiling without any rancor. Of course she knew his preferences and knew them better than almost anyone else.

She didn't hear him. "Dear?"

"Come in, Mrs. Lloyd."

She entered, wearing a thick dressing gown of faded fern green. "Oh, perfect, you've kept it warm in here." She did so worry for him.

"I'm not a monk."

"I do know that." The tea tray she carried went on his desk with a clatter, and he sat up again. He couldn't see her expression, but her words carried a slight smile. "I thought you might be awake."

"So, you thought I would be awake and I would want some tea."

"I saw how you gazed at that man. The new one. The one who came to visit you."

"He didn't come to visit me."

Not for the first time, he was incredibly aware of how Mrs. Lloyd was more worldly, more understanding, than she appeared. On her exterior, she looked like any other woman from the streets of his childhood, approachable in a beautiful, not-to-be crossed way, clad in knit woolens and old tweed and generally bearing a smile. But she was eerily knowledgeable of what was generally afoot. She knew the unspoken currents that other people often missed because she herself possessed hidden depths.

"Did he not?"

"If he did for the reason your voice implies," said Tom, aiming for droll and securing black humor, "we would be brought to trial and possibly imprisoned."

"Never! You're not wealthy enough. Don't have the right accent, either."

Tom chuckled and ran a hand through his hair. Always hopelessly awry, he could control it with a hat of the appropriate kind for the given situation. Caps favored by working men were ideal, as he rarely needed to remove them while he was out and about. Anything made of straw always escaped from his head; bowlers weren't something he liked. "Thank you for that perspective."

She handed him a cup of sweetened tea at a perfect temperature, and it warmed the body without scalding the tongue. He held it carefully as Mrs. Lloyd settled in the single chair in his room, shifting the timetables to rest next to the tea tray before she did so. "Planning a journey, then?"

"Only a short one."

"It's been an age since you've been into the city."

"I thought I'd see Gran. Bring some flowers to the grave."

"And your mother?"

"If her husband will have me."

"Of course he will."

"I think he, ah, knows." He had not told Mother, yet Mother knew, too. But it was quite another matter for a man who was essentially a stranger to him to know. He could not say precisely how Mr. Peel might have learned the truth, for he was neither ostentatious in his pursuits nor was he a dandy who left his identity legible for the sake of attracting suitors. Not that all dandies were inverts.

But Peel always looked at him distrustfully, sharply, and when he spoke, his words matched the wariness in his eyes. It was an unpleasant experience and Tom did not leave himself open to sensing what Peel might be emanating emotionally. Enforcing that boundary, unfortunately, took effort. Much like clinging to rigging in a storm.

Tom took a sip of tea, letting it warm his irritated throat. In great contrast to Peel, Mrs. Lloyd was a familiar presence, one whose feelings he could navigate because he knew her. He did not feel as though he was on the fringes of madness when he gleaned her happiness, her dismay, her vexation.

Now he felt her serenity. It certainly did not originate from him.

"The world is not always a terrible place," she said. "Things are changing. They will change even more, given time. So what if he does know, then?"

He pondered that. Perhaps there was something to not caring, as well as to the idea he was not wealthy enough for difference to matter. "I don't know."

"Surely you don't believe you're an abomination." She did not brook argument.

"Not for that." He laughed a little. "Fine, you harridan. If it doesn't matter, do you think Theo—" He had his own opinions and only wanted to know if what he assumed, and felt, might be visible to another person. Mrs. Lloyd knew him well, and she also would not lie to spare his feelings.

"Theo, hm? Is that short for Theodore?" She would veer in the direction of full, delighted teasing if he was not careful.

Without any spite, he said, "Hold your peace." Then, he added, "I don't imagine there would be any other name it is short for. Yes. The one who *visited* today. Do you think he knows?"

"Water is wet." She arched an eyebrow. "He'd have had you on the bar if I hadn't come with that tray."

Tom swallowed, banishing the visceral sensations brought by her words. "I see. That, I rather didn't catch."

Perhaps it did not matter if Theo had come to see him. Besides what he knew of the matter, it was evident, or evident enough for men who couldn't be more overt than they were, that David had some claim on Theo. He winced just a little, and Mrs. Lloyd was quick to see it even in the shifting firelight.

"What is it?"

"You. . . he. . . may. . . David came, too."

"Mr. Mills?"

"Yes."

"Your David?"

"He's not mine and if he was, I wouldn't want him now."

A graceful finger tapped thin lips as Mrs. Lloyd considered the matter. "You mean to say, David came to The Shuck because Theo was here."

It was an odd pairing, but Tom had seen odder examples. David was far too rigid, formal, moneyed, and Theo was none of those things. Well, he might be moneyed.

Stop. It doesn't bear thinking about anything he might be.

"It seemed as though he was not pleased to see Theo here," said Tom, "but as to any of his motivations, I'm not entirely certain."

The encounter had been so tense it was part of the reason why he'd felt a strong need to visit the city. Just the idea that all three of them were knocking about the same small vicinity was going to drive him to distraction. Everything else, on the other hand, had driven him to drink. He had far too many questions and too few answers.

A rational and learned man would claim there was no fate and maybe no God, but the way Theo was present at a time Tom had chosen specifically for its desolation was almost elegant and nearly by design. He was certain, as well, that many men would leave someone to their whims, especially a drunk, and more especially someone who so adamantly wished to expire.

He didn't want to consider himself so surly, and that was too close to what his uncle might be termed when he was in a foul mood, but Tom had to admit his own unpleasant demeanor was another reason why many other people might not want to get involved with his distress.

"Leaving Mr. Mills to one side," said Mrs. Lloyd, "Theo, if I may call him such because you do, was plainly present to see *you*. What happened the night you came in all wet, dear?" Her eyes drifted to his neck where it met his shoulder, where he'd developed something of a long bruise from where Theo had been supporting all of his weight in the water. He'd been unconscious, naturally, so he didn't know how long he'd been held that way, but it didn't take long for a body to bruise.

She didn't mean during their strange shared spread, the one that had him feeling electrified or enraged depending on the given moment. She meant before it occurred. He glanced up from his tea and met her eyes. As ever, they were impossibly kind.

"You cannot tell my uncle."

"There is a great deal I do not put to your uncle."

"It will not please you, either." Wary, he sipped.

"I have known you since you were a boy. Of course it will not please me. I wish for you to be happy and I know you are not, so I shall not be pleased until I see such a thing."

With certainty, he knew she spoke the truth. He could not think of anyone else who had said something similar to him. "I went for a walk to the water."

It was all he had to say.

He drank the rest of his cup, she refilled it after he held it out, and the silence between them became nearly tactile.

Then she spoke. "You did not wish to come back."

"Theo did not listen to that."

"And yet you think he didn't come here to see you," she said.

He appreciated she didn't ask why he did not wish to come back, or profess shock, or act as though he should be ashamed of himself or incarcerated for his own good. A small wave of shame did visit him when he suspected she would likely think more about his revelation later and allow herself to feel poorly about it in privacy. He could not deny that she looked after him as she would a son.

Better than many sons were looked after. He thought fleetingly of David's father.

Then much of the attempt and its aftermath returned to him, unbidden, and he blinked, staring at his own eyes in the surface of the tea. "I don't know how he managed it. I kept in mind the wind, the temperature, the tide."

I should have died, he did not add.

"But he did," she said.

"Yes." With a kiss. Or, at least, that was the first thing he could recall after the cold darkness. *Not that it was really a kiss.* It was hardly a real kiss if it was just to save his life.

"And he returned you here."

"Yes."

"Did you not wish to invite him up?"

"Mrs. Lloyd!"

She said it innocently enough, but there was playfulness in the turn of her smile. "I might have, myself, had I been a little younger."

"Oh, hush. If I had, then we would really have had to keep Paul unaware of a great many things."

"He would not care. Can't keep quiet, then, can you?"

Less shocked than amused, Tom chuckled. A woman who'd once made pleasure her trade would make such a quip and many of her prior clients had to have passed away by now. Benson had once been one of them, according to her, but he did not seem to know his left from his right on most days.

Tom also did not wish to picture him sleeping the night with anybody.

"Whether or not I can keep quiet when I choose to *unite* with another isn't pertinent. And I'll have you know, I have managed a great many decadent things incredibly quietly."

She smirked and leaned over to pat his arm with her free hand. "There's your smile. But, truly, your uncle is still unwell. I don't suppose anything would rouse him before he rouses himself."

"Any change?"

She was the only person Paul would tolerate in his rooms and he would not allow them to summon a doctor, not even Dr. Jones, with whom he was friendly. In part, this had to be because his illness was not one of the body and could not be cured. "He is talking more, but if you wished to travel, I would just do so soon. You lingering here and skulking about improves very little for your uncle. Rather, I should say there is nothing you can do for him."

"And if he passes, I shall need to run the place." He knew he shouldn't sound so dour and probably needed to be thankful for the livelihood being left to him. "Won't have much time to travel, then." Thankfulness was a difficult thing to accomplish, if only because he could not quite imagine living into the next month, never mind imagining what the next year might be like. The weight of his inability to do so drove him to excesses.

"I don't know that I would say he's any closer to the grave. But you could sell it, of course," she said. "If you really cannot abide the thought." There was no judgement in her words, only practicality. He peered at her. "I expect it would fetch a sound price."

"What would you do?"

"I could find something."

He was unconvinced but appreciated her support. He supposed she could return to Norwich, but nothing she had said suggested she had any family. There was always the possibility of another guesthouse or inn taking her as a housekeeper, as she did have a stalwart reputation. But then he thought of Benson, who would probably not be taken in anywhere else even though he came up with his rent every week, and Benson was just one of their lodgers at various points in the year.

The thing that put Tom out about taking his uncle's place was precisely that he had to remember he was looking after others, many of whom were on the edges of what society deemed worthy anyway. They were not vile or what he would call worthless, but he knew he did not align with the majority in almost any of his perceptions.

Then again, Paul managed to keep things running most of the time and he was not boundlessly altruistic, just ethical in his own odd way. Despite everything and despite how he acted around his nephew, he seemed admirably accepting of humanity's complexities. It was this period from Christmas to Valentine's Day or so that posed the most difficulty for him.

Regardless, he was never the landlord or innkeeper who pounded on doors demanding money a day after it was due.

Of course not. He is Miss Havisham, not Mr. Scrooge. But she was more tragic, he felt, even if the world was filled with Scrooges who bred tragedy.

12

While David had a slightly calculating mind that could be common in men who had money and property, Theo wasn't quite familiar with the intensity that bloomed after they'd shared a drink with Tom in the taproom. Or at least, he felt the hawkish change in attitude was related to the meeting. It was hard to say and he did try to edge away from David's distrust, markedly avoiding their custom of casual chatter while still attempting to remain affable, which probably seemed strange anyway. He was more acquiescent when they played cards or chess, less likely to try winning just for the fun of it. While he still made soft quips, he was sure not to be too clever in his delivery. He wanted to keep his distance like a man respecting a massive bonfire, and hoped it would die down a little.

He trusted it would, he just didn't want to hazard a guess at when. It was clear Tom had roused some tension in David.

When he calmed, Theo could speak to him sensibly, tell him the truth of his intentions and what he envisioned for their future, which was to say that it would diverge.

Theo scowled. A few days and nights of smoldering but smothering surveillance was enough to make him decide he would leave as soon as he could. He had very few affairs to put in order and almost no one to say good-bye to, so it stood to reason he could manage a disappearance of a sort. As a child, he'd heard tell of some of his ilk who'd faked their deaths to move on, but he was not nearly so extreme. It was an option, he supposed, but not one he would ever favor unless he somehow had to.

He walked through a little lane opposite a cheese monger and a small stationery shop whose musty air he could smell from outside, deep in thought about the most efficient way to accomplish his escape. His skin was what mattered most and he had that, so he *could* simply leave David a note and depart. He did not want to. David was not the friend with whom he wished to live out his years—or, to be morbid, the friend whom he wished to watch age and ultimately die—but neither could he simply abandon the man.

Wandering while so pensive took him to part of town he did not know.

These rows of cottages were charming, but after a few minutes, he had to admit he was turned around, even though it seemed hard to believe. The sea helped him adjust slightly, but apart from understanding where *it* was, he could not make a guess where *he* was.

"That rather takes it," he said to no one at all. He'd told David he was only posting a letter. If this took any time deemed to be over the appropriate amount for such a chore, he would grow suspicious.

He was preoccupied while gazing at the church tower, trying to deduce the best way back, when he made out grunting. No, shouts. At first, he thought it could be an altercation. The noise was muffled through the modest window just opposite him. The street was quite narrow.

Then he smirked to himself when he understood the noises for what they were. *Moaning, not shouts.* The law had little bearing on pleasure between grown men. Irresistibly, he was drawn to the window, where the curtains were sensibly closed and only a small space between them allowed a little light through.

He wasn't the sort who'd spy on intimacies, so part of him was embarrassed that his feet seemed to be moving of their own accord. Still, driven by the same heat that had bloomed under his palm when he rested it on Tom's arm, waiting for him to stop coughing, he carefully looked.

What he saw was enough to keep him riveted, even as his rational thoughts turned to fleeing. One man was not in any position at all to see an interloper at the window. The second man, who silently and unwittingly beckoned him to stay, was not unknown to him.

Tom was splayed on a small bed in such a way that, should he open his eyes, he might notice the intrusion. The glass was old and dirty, the curtains thick where they were drawn, but the possibility was present.

Yet Theo could not bring himself to do the decent thing until the last possible moment, when Tom's companion shifted and Tom wrenched his eyes open, smiling. It was not the purest smile Theo had ever seen on his face, but it was full of pleasure.

Suddenly, Theo coveted it, much as he coveted the muscles that moved under his skin and the flush of his cheeks. He came away from the window knowing he had not been seen, but almost wishing he'd been spotted.

~

THEIR ENCOUNTER WAS WELL ENOUGH by Tom's standards, exactly what he'd been after and what he'd needed to drive out an excess of energy. Since he'd had most of his in cramped bunks and rooms above public houses, even a small bed in an old cottage was almost luxurious.

Anyway, luxury did not always mean luxurious. After all, one notable time in David's father's house, which was luxurious to a fault, had changed the course of his life. But he supposed that was inevitable given his inclinations. Tom had never been with David in Cambridge. *Because you were not a student,* he thought.

That wouldn't have been the right kind of almost-public liaison for Mr. David Mills. He mostly assumed David did not wish to be associated with what his peers might term a bit of rough. Hell, David might have called him that, too, outside of his hearing. Always aspirational, always fastidious, David would want his known partners to suit his own place in the world.

Like Theo, who seemed enigmatic but genteel. But Tom noticed how the light had changed, and told himself a vague knowledge of the time and his responsibilities was what cooled his enthusiasm for the man draped over him.

It wasn't. A few moments ago, that blasted *presence* he associated only with Theo was *there* like a full moon behind clouds. He couldn't see him and the curtains weren't even open, but that didn't matter. He was there, somewhere outside, and there was no pretending he wasn't.

Will, of course, assumed Tom's completion was the

result of his own carnal prowess. Since Will was not an arrogant soul, but just a simple one, Tom let him feel smug. There was no manner in which Tom could explain the unspoken connections he made to people that would not sound like folly, anyway. He had never tried, choosing instead to try to blunt them with alcohol, overwork, reading novels whose titles he had to obscure — what man chose the gothic and romantic, or fairy tales, as his pet genres — and wandering about. Since he did not see himself reflected in the world as most of its inhabitants explained it, he looked elsewhere for comfort and meaning and found them within the fantastical.

Alongside that, he moved about to distract himself from what he lacked.

He stared at the veins in Will's neck, becoming gradually aware Will was speaking and not just breathing. "I'd heard you were back, but it didn't seem the done thing to come find you," said Will.

Privately, Tom agreed. He did not like being sought out and had always thought he would not want to be. Then Theo's brown eyes came to mind—he knew he would welcome Theo in that case. "I've been busy at The Shuck."

"Even now?"

"My uncle hasn't been well." Not everyone knew about Paul's utter inability to cope with this time of year. Will was one such person. Tom suspected there was still gossip about Mr. Apollyon's odd habits, but outside of his intimate acquaintances and family, no one was privy to all of the exact details. Which, if the details were as Mrs. Lloyd had said, was a blessing.

"That explains it," said Will, looking down at Tom with his easy smile framed by deep dimples. They had come together several times in the last year or two.

Will owned the cottage that had been his grandfather's and his father's, and he remained without a family of his own, preferring instead to live alone. He used the cyclical nature of his work to justify his bachelorhood to his elderly aunt who lived in Overstrand and sometimes came to visit her errant nephew. She complained about his lack of children upon every visit.

Really, it was a shame that Will would probably never marry, for even though Tom had never seen him with children, it was easy to imagine him enjoying fatherhood and being patient with them. Will was jovial and kind, as well as amenable to something casual and sporadic. His hands were roughened by years of fishing and he was built like a Spartan, or what Tom imagined a Spartan would have looked like, at any rate. It should have been a perfect arrangement and in many ways it was.

But he did not set Tom's heart stuttering as Theo did. Not just Theo, but Theo's—*whatever precedes him, wherever he goes,* thought Tom.

Everyone had something of the kind, but Theo's translated to delicate champagne bubbles and starlight refracted off seawater. Mrs. Lloyd was the scent of fresh honey and she emanated steel-smooth equilibrium; Paul had strong birch-tar loyalty and also suggested cinnamon's warmth, which actually made Tom more tolerant of his dark moods. A bad man, he'd realized long ago, wouldn't feel that way to him.

"Explains what?" Tom asked, at last.

"Why I haven't seen you."

"Wait, did you miss... me?"

Will could not have truly missed him; they did not have that kind of relationship, or so Tom thought. But there was more than fondness in Will's eyes when he said, "I wished to see you."

"For this?"

Will smoothed some hair from Tom's forehead. It was an unexpectedly gentle gesture, and Tom tried not to go tense as it was delivered. "Well, yes."

But poor Will must not have been as straightforward a person as Tom assumed, for he smiled ruefully, seeming to infer the reason for the change in Tom's posture. "I should let you go. I imagine Mrs. Lloyd may need your help. How does she do, these days?" He shifted over him, then came away from the bed, righting his clothes. The cold seeped into Tom's bones quickly, as did a touch of regret that he'd caused Will any pain. He'd misunderstood the extent of his regard, it seemed.

Rather than apologize, for he couldn't find the right words, he sat up, fixing his shirt and doing up his trousers. "She's well. She's happy to fuss over me."

"If you let her."

"Pardon?"

"If you let her fuss. You ought to let someone, you know." Will eyed him with lingering desire, but crossed his arms as though reminding himself not to touch Tom.

Trying to keep an arch tone, Tom said, realizing the mess he'd presently made of especially his shirt, "I shall have to explain why I need warm water in the middle of the day."

"Warm water? You *have* become used to comforts, haven't you?"

He smirked up at Will as he put on his boots. "I thought you'd just said I should let someone fuss over me."

"Not if it means rousing suspicion. Asking for warm water in the late afternoon might."

"Mrs. Lloyd would never take issue. Even if she knew, which, as far as my preferences are concerned, she does." Not that it felt at all like a preference. He wouldn't want to prefer something that was so precarious and often difficult.

Disbelief showed in Will's frown. Tom stood and kissed him on the cheek. "You... she..."

"Don't worry yourself. She's tighter than wax," said Tom. Her background was not his to divulge, so he wouldn't, but he wanted to add that she of all people would understand the need for discretion.

Will softened under the kiss, just as Tom knew he would. "I should know *you* wouldn't trust just anyone."

The words still rang in his ears after he'd taken his leave of Will's cottage and stepped outside, exiting the small enclave of pleasure for the quiet lane outside. While he didn't mind Will believing him to be a suspicious man because it perhaps simplified their situation—who would want to make a long companion of a man prone to suspicion, after all—it did hurt.

As he buttoned his coat, he became aware the champagne and starlight hadn't gone far away at all. Part of him, one he did not allow often to the fore, set out to look for it.

13

Sunlight had dissipated from the sky, yet Theo still lurked in the lane. He couldn't bring himself to leave. No logic or reason would sway him, not David's potential ire, not decency or respect for Tom's privacy. He told himself he was still lost, but truly he just did not want to put his mind to finding his way back and hoped someone would find him before he did.

His mind, the traitorous thing, was fixed on Tom and precisely his face as he neared pleasure. His hope, another traitorous thing, was fastened to the thought he'd be able to catch Tom on his way back to the inn. Meanwhile, his heart was caught between his mind and his hope. It knew, though it could not provide evidence, he and Tom could make a very good go of things.

To what end, he didn't know. It didn't seem to matter, but some things one just knew. *You are too old to behave like this.* He should be too old and too wily. Not to mention, the act he had just witnessed was illegal. He should not covet it and certainly, he should not allow himself to keep entertaining thoughts of Tom. *Especially if you wish to leave.*

He rounded a corner and, eyes on his shoes, walked directly into a firm mass. The mass grunted and put steady palms on his upper arms to keep him from stumbling back and losing his footing.

"My apologies, I—"

"David lives some distance from here." Tom sounded less surprised than Theo would have expected. This was a small place, but it wasn't tiny and it was popular enough, so seeing acquaintances was not always a given event.

Theo looked up.

Tom had sounded, mercifully and maddeningly, charmed. Almost resigned, even. He *looked* well-bedded, which was not something Theo wanted to notice but did and would have even if he had not lurked at a strange window to confirm the perception. "Hello, Mr. Drunkard."

"You may be stupendous in water, but you have no sense of direction on land, do you? His house can't be reached this way at all."

"That's not a strictly accurate assumption. . ." Theo licked his lower lip. Tom's gaze followed his tongue for just a moment, which made him smug, then it resettled on his eyes. "I was thinking while I was walking and found myself abstracted. Some parts I know well enough, but. . ."

"I don't imagine David keeps company in many fishermen's cottages. I doubt any member of the Mills family has set foot around here. Too uncouth. Possibly too many sights to offend the eye and one's finer sensibilities."

Theo didn't think Tom realized he was gently squeezing his arms and rubbing them absently like he was petting a soft, nervous cat. Rather than risk stopping that action, Theo chuckled and said, "You may be right. Or. . ." He thought better of it. "Perhaps David has, for I have no notion of what he got up to before meeting me."

Snorting, Tom assured him, "Nothing around here."

Theo said, "So. . . you and he. . ." The air in the tap-room had been stodgier than a Christmas pudding. He didn't really need to ask Tom the truth of it, only it seemed the prudent and polite thing to do under the circumstances. He cleared his throat. "You and he. . ."

"A while ago, now."

"How long ago?"

"Long before you would have met him."

"I wasn't terribly concerned about that," said Theo, wishing he could explain his rather unorthodox grasp on the idea of relationships. Or anything at all. With the tenets of modern science well on the rise and in-fluencing even the most commonplace of men, it was hard to say who would think he was spitting non-sense, or who might take him in earnest, or who might want to lock him away, or who might laugh.

"We were so young and thoughtless. We kept meeting until his second summer back from Cam-bridge. He was different, then, before he took up the family trade. If you like him now, you'd certainly like him better then."

Theo dodged that statement. He wasn't sure. "Did you go to university?"

Tom glanced at him, then held up his hands with a jolly grin. Even in the gloaming and the worsening sky, Theo spied a gorgeous collage of callouses and scars. A few of his fingers looked like they had been broken, for they were slightly crooked. "Do these look like a student's hands, my good lad?"

"Ah, no, not to put too fine a point on it." Although

they didn't look pampered or soft, Theo tamped down the desire to say something asinine about wanting to feel them anyway. "What's that one from?" He nodded to a long scar on Tom's left thumb.

"Bit of glass on the floor. A regular patron of my uncle's became rowdy, threw a bottle, and in my haste to clean things up, I didn't see all of the shards. One sliced me. I think I was thirteen? My sense of time is a little warped when I try to think back... they must be right about some of the things drink does to the mind."

Feeling audacious indeed, Theo reached out and touched it lightly with his right thumb. "Must have bled profusely. Hands always do. My father was an apothecary and people would often come to him for wounds." He forgot men like his father weren't always called *an apothecary* in England these days, but let it pass without amending the word. "Sometimes even if they needed a surgeon or a doctor, and especially if they were too poor for the latter." Tom did not draw his thumb away, but his breath hitched once before it steadied again. If anything, he pressed his thumb into Theo's, which roused a proprietary self-assuredness.

"There was a shocking amount of blood. Looked like someone had been murdered. Ah... what were we discussing?"

"University."

"I left school with no inclination to go anywhere but elsewhere. Preferably on a boat. I grew up in Norwich, you see. But Paul had The Shuck and I'd often seen the fishermen and the tradesmen when I came to visit." He smiled. "I don't know. I do love to read and I'm always thinking about things, not that I look like the sort, but schooling didn't fit me. I had no desire to be a clerk, my family is nowhere near politics, no one has gone to university. . . we're not poor, certainly not destitute. . . but we all must work." He appeared to think, and added, "And I rarely had the ability to concentrate on my lessons."

"Very practical of you."

"If I wasn't working in a pub, I took work on the docks, and fished, and hauled things about for people wealthier than me. No university in there at all. What about you? Did you ever want to attend?"

"Oh, I. . ." He could tell the truth, but that would require a delineation of *when,* and when would turn into *how.* Theo knew that they did not live more than a century or possibly two beyond what was considered a human lifespan, which did not seem like an enormous amount of time to him, yet it did pose its own issues. Even the most stalwart of souls would find it difficult to grasp the disparity between his appearance and actual age. He teetered on the verge of saying he had attended university about twenty years ago while he was still living in Edinburgh, although he looked to be in his thirties at a push. He decided not to mention that he was almost a century old. He could at a later time, but now was not the moment.

"You don't have to be ashamed if you didn't," said Tom, misinterpreting his silence. "I only assumed that's how David would meet someone."

"But he didn't meet *you* at university," Theo said. This fellow was sweeter than he looked, if he was telling him not to feel shame over a lack of education.

"No. He first met me in the taproom and convinced me to bring him a pint. About a year after I sliced my thumb on that bit of the bottle Toothless Rob had chucked." Tom shook his head. "It's looking murderous out. I can walk you back. Don't say you can find your way." He grinned.

"I don't know if that would be a good idea. He might be out and about."

"Oh, fuck him," said Tom dismissively. "The puffed-up popinjay."

Theo laughed and did not say, *You have*. "Really, Mr. Apollyon?"

"Pardon me. He cannot be everywhere at once, you know. And though he might believe he is God, he lacks God's supposed omnipotence."

"I haven't any idea of what you mean."

"Coy doesn't suit you," Tom said. "David is a kitten pretending to be a lion. I don't think he was cuddled enough as a child."

"He wasn't cuddled at all, if you hear his side of things."

The only answer to that was a low, affirmative grunt. "You met his father, so I assume you can imagine why that is so."

"Thankfully, I didn't see him much. Only when I've come to Cromer, and that's just been for Christmas until Twelfth Night or early February at most. David never seems to enjoy the thought of summers here, which is odd, because it really would be the best time to come. And the senior Mr. Mills was quite. . ." Theo scrunched his nose as he considered his words, trying to phrase it gently. "His mind was not intact, especially in his last days." Having been with David during those last days did make it harder to leave him, now. It almost felt like taking one more thing from him.

They were starting down a gentle incline and could see more of the beach, now, but he kept sneaking looks at Tom. His coloring was much better than it had been and his eyes were clearer. It was irresistible to think of why he seemed so alive, and relentlessly, Theo told himself to keep to the moment at hand.

Many would say he should be disgusted that Tom was slightly sweaty in the way one might be if they ran a low fever. His speech was somehow easier. He was clearly more relaxed. But far from being disgusted, Theo was now more intrigued than ever. Some jealousy lingered there, too, but he tried to parry it with rationality. He was seeing David and in many respects they were living like man and wife. That should keep him on one path and even if he wished to leave, he should have a care to doing that like a gentleman.

He shouldn't be so drawn to this cantankerous lad who bore gentleness hidden like veins of gold in dark earth. To make matters worse, every few moments, he had a whiff of something he would have sworn was a Guerlain scent, only no person with Tom's history—who he'd ever met, anyway—would have worn such an extravagant thing. It must have been costly. It wove itself in with the breeze and the cold salt, intriguing and lingering.

"Your cologne," said Theo. "It's different. What is it?"

Tom bit his lip. He said, "You can't tell anyone."

"I wouldn't dream of it."

"It's Jicky," Tom said. He tilted his head and distrust loomed in his eyes. "I've never told anybody. Then again, nobody has remarked upon it."

Although Theo wanted to reassure him that it smelled sublime, he refrained from saying any such thing. "I see."

"My gran, my mother's mother, received it as a gift and I just liked it, so I tried some one day and kept the habit. It doesn't smell the same on me as it did on her, though. Strange how that works."

"It suits you. Lavender, I suppose, suits you."

Quietly, with a note of disgrace, Tom said, "I like the vanilla, too."

Theo looked at him, hoping his own expression wasn't too soft. "It still suits you." He paused, then asked, "So, you grew up in Norwich. But your uncle keeps an establishment here. Ah, and David. . . often did the same. . . traveled back and forth?"

Tom smiled and gave a quiet laugh. "More or less. Yes. I was always here during summers. David. . . I know he is from Norwich, too, but I rarely visited him there." He took a few steps, quiet. "My mother and father felt it would be good for me to be near the sea when I could be, and they were right. I loved it. I suppose David would not want to risk crossing paths with me now, if I had my guess. Might be nervous about what I'd do. But I've never wanted anything from him. Not money, or. . . anything." He stepped over a cobblestone that had come loose. "And it would not have mattered to me, seeing him. He has always been more leery of me."

Theo found himself listing nearer to him as they walked, drawn by the urbane fragrance and the gentle laugh. "Because you broke things off?"

"No. Truth all told, I did not take them as seriously as he did, I think. But I didn't break anything off," said Tom. He sighed and looked at Theo, who did his best not to look too intently at his face. "He did. Well, his father did. His father caught us the once in bed. So if he had you around his father and in his father's house, that must mean he cares for you. It was. . . not pleasant. I mean to say, Mr. Mills didn't lift a hand against either of us, but he did shout. I didn't know he had it in him." His mouth lifted in a half-smile. "If you met him, I do think David must. . . esteem you."

"I think he does," said Theo cautiously. It was hard to gauge, for David was not a bad man or even a deeply covetous one, but Theo had the sense he often did not understand his own feelings and clung to things out of fear rather than love or affection.

"After that, after we were discovered, I mean, David did everything he could to distance himself from me. Well. . . first he thought we could secretly make a go of it, but. . . oh, best not to tell you what he said. We all say silly things when we're boys." Tom pulled a face of disdain. "But, I suspect Mr. Mills might have threatened to disown David, perhaps to do more than that. He neither disavowed or accused me publicly, however, which I appreciate."

It wouldn't be beyond all possibility that Mr. Mills would have considered disowning his only son. Theo did not know him well in the manner a friend of the family would, as he had only met him in the midst of his declining health. He was supposedly an imperious fellow and a religious one. Despite those qualities, he was not entirely within his wits when Theo was introduced to him, which was probably why David felt comfortable conducting a longer and more serious association under his father's narrow nose.

The suggestion that Mr. Mills might have considered legal actions against his own son seemed extreme. And sad. His father would never. After his mother had left them, Father hadn't been keen on alienating Theo in any way and had doted on him. "Wouldn't that have brought attention to it?"

"What?"

"Doing. . . more than disowning him."

"Oh, I see what you mean. Indeed. I don't mean to suggest he'd have gone to the courts and brought disgrace to the family. He was far too protective of his assets and their name." Tom pulled his hat lower against the wind. "But, you see, if David had been disowned, he wouldn't have had any means at all, so after his savings became thin and disappeared, where would he go? What would he do?"

Silent, Theo nodded.

"I think, before he became a feeble old man, he would have seen no problem with allowing his son to suffer. After that summer, I rarely saw David. When I did, I never saw him with other lads, but I often heard he was courting some miss or another. I think he must hold me a little responsible for ruining his life, at least for some time."

"There was a woman before me," said Theo. "It was like watching a man with sand in his tea instead of sugar."

Tom's lips quirked into a smile. "I can imagine." He tilted his head. "How did you meet, then? Go on, I've told you how we met."

"Well, it was nowhere near as dramatic as rescuing him from the sea, I will say."

"David would rather cut his nose off than give into hysterics. He used to say I was too overemotional even before he wasn't allowed to see me."

"That's not very kind of him." Theo shook his head. "Ah, he'd just taken on his father's responsibilities with the business and he needed a secretary, so I applied. We weren't always. . . it wasn't always the kind of. . . arrangement it is now. Of course, we. . . it is good subterfuge, but I actually am his secretary." In a way, talking about all this felt liberating. He so rarely could speak of it in the open.

"Sensible."

"Where. . . are you taking me?"

"We're going the long way," said Tom.

It shouldn't have pleased him as much as it did. "Oh. Good. I like the scenery here." That, at least, he did not mean as a sly come-hither invitation. He found it lovely, truly.

"I don't suppose it's much compared to where you've been, but it is beautiful."

After a chuckle, Theo said, "That again. I don't know *how* I don't sound like I *should*"—and he resented being asked why he spoke as he did, though could never put his finger on why he resented it—"but as I said, I have lived other places."

He could hazard a guess the way he sounded was to do with his age or an adaptability that others might have lacked. That was, like so many other facets of his life, something he could not discuss much or at all. Better to seem a roguish, educated drifter than rouse suspicions that might lead to his incarceration in a cell at a police station. *Or a laboratory. Or an asylum.*

Still, he had wanted for quite some time to find someone to live his life with, to keep him, to trust someone with whom he could share all the facets and fragments of his life. He wondered if he was naïve for waiting for such a thing, but when he was near Tom, he felt he was not.

That might have been more naïve. They'd shared no more than a few conversations.

Marriages are often built on less, he thought.

On the other hand, he and David had had many business meetings, then many clandestine, far less-businesslike meetings, before he'd committed to co-habitating with the man. None of it was stopping the quiet, steadfast erosion of their relationship.

"Oh, I'm not going to prod you about the way you talk. I'm pure Norwich when I open my mouth. I shouldn't be making light of anyone's speech."

He grew more contrite, for he saw that Tom was not going to make anything of it, not even in the way David did under the pretense of good-natured teasing. It wasn't teasing at all when David did it. "How I *sound* comes up in conversation, often, and I always have to justify myself."

"I won't require you to. I was only saying this coast is pretty, but I prefer the north's coasts. They're not all more drastic, but I do find I like the striking ones."

"You think I'd prefer something drastic?"

His arch, little remark had Tom blushing, not that he could entirely tell under all the stubble or the tan that winter had slightly faded. But Theo could surmise from the way his eyes dropped for a second before he looked ahead. Then Tom said, "I have not known you long at all, but I don't think I'd presume to tell you what you preferred."

Theo brought a finger to Tom's wrist and kindly tapped it. Tom blinked, looking at him, apparently surprised by another bit of minute contact. "Maybe you could." Then, spooked by his own temerity, Theo let his finger drop. "I thought of a story you might like, the other night." *The other night while David was sleeping half-draped over me, and I had to think about other things to fall asleep myself.*

"A ghost story?"

"Of sorts." Theo smiled. It was most relevant to him. Tom might not appreciate it as much. But when he'd recalled it from the many stories his father enjoyed telling him before bedtime or to pass a dreich afternoon, the way in which they had met became eerily appropriate.

14

P aul's second intact sentence to Tom in the space of about one week was, "You were seen." The words were accompanied by the normal phantom birch tar and a sulfuric undertone that felt new. He didn't know what it might connote, precisely, but the same thing had happened sometimes when he knew someone felt under the weather.

Tom's nose twitched, even though he was still generally certain and had been for years that the smells weren't of the world. They weren't the sort of thing one discussed, because they might say disastrous things about the state of one's mind. He looked up from his book and set it to the side, careful to put the cover face-down. He didn't think he could manage not to shout if Paul said something scathing about the brothers Grimm, and he was drawn too taut to respond with much equilibrium to his uncle's disparagements.

"Good morning to you, too."

Not allowing Paul to make him feel like a chastised boy, he sat up straight on his made bed and crossed his arms. He was too old for *you were seen* to spark much alarm and anyway, he knew for a fact there was no way he could have been seen with Will. They'd been in his home—which was his alone—and they'd been discreet, *and* Will was fully trustworthy. They certainly knew how to comport themselves and he hadn't done anything else worth *seeing*. Absolutely not in the last several days, at least.

Which wasn't to say he hadn't been thinking about doing those kinds of things with Theo to the point of mild distraction. It didn't have an effect on what he accomplished. Actually, it seemed to galvanize him.

He'd chosen new curtains, sent away two tufted benches to be reupholstered, and finally negotiated better prices with their greengrocers.

Part of the negotiations had to do with bribing the wife and husband pair with some of the excellent whisky they had on offer. Grocers were never above being bribed and he knew for a fact their competitors had already bribed for the first pick of the day. Even if anyone wished to deny they had done it, it was obvious from the delivery times.

He could not compete on that level and still provide a decent salary for Mrs. Lloyd and himself, so he resorted to the next best thing and had proven successful.

Though he was recovered enough to resume his duties, Paul had not deigned to utter much in the course of taking up his work again. Instead, he conveyed answers to direct questions with one or two words and if he noticed developments with the greengrocers, the new curtains, or the reupholstered benches, he didn't say.

He'd come downstairs at midmorning days ago, surprising Mrs. Lloyd, Tom, and Benson, who was underfoot just as he had been since Boxing Day or so.

"What ho," said Benson, "what ho, sir!"

Mrs. Lloyd seemed to think he was talking to men they could not see, again, which he often did. Her eyes laughed as she looked at Tom. Little harm was in it and Benson rarely became agitated unless he was asked to stop, so neither Tom nor Mrs. Lloyd challenged him.

They'd arrived at the silent but important agreement that it was better not to question his perceptions, which were clearly real enough to him.

But Tom, knowing the eddy in the air for who it suggested, had looked to the stairs and met his uncle's eyes. He and Paul had similar eyes, eyes like Father's, though Paul's were closer to green than hazel unless he wore brown tones that the hazel might pick up.

Now Paul's eyes were dark, with nights of little sleep smudged in purpled skin under them.

"Good morning, Benson," Paul said, his voice a disused rumble.

"Good morning, Mr. Apollyon," said Mrs. Lloyd.

He offered her the smallest of genuine smiles. "Mrs. Lloyd."

Paul and Tom had simply nodded at each other. He did not know what else to say, for he was glad to see his uncle despite everything, while still nervous he might choose the wrong words to say so. That simple nodding would continue, it transpired, with just a few variations, including *yes* and *no*. There was not very much to be said from a business perspective because all had gone smoothly. Though, Paul *had* thanked him for his good work and Tom then had to check he was not dreaming by prodding his own palm with the tip of his pen. Not enough to hurt, just enough to produce some physical sensation and leave a small stain.

Tom knew what he would have been doing for days in his room, but Paul didn't drink much. Whatever had been eating at him, it was purely of the heart and was not induced or numbed by artificial means. There were so many questions Tom wanted to ask and didn't. Namely, he wanted to know more about Alistair, but such requests probably would have made little impact when Paul was not forthcoming with anything else.

It was lucky he already knew his way around bookkeeping as well as the daily chores one needed to do to maintain an inn or a pub, or he might be lost without any explanations or conversations from the proprietor himself.

He took a breath and gazed at Paul in the doorway, waiting for him to speak more than those three caustic words.

He merely exchanged them for three new caustic words. "Good morning, indeed."

"What do you mean, I was seen?"

"With that dandified secretary of Mr. Mills'—that one who comes with him around this time of year. I usually notice him in town because he leaves a trail of interested parties in his wake." In the offing was the precise, actual nature of the secretarial relationship.

Tom sighed. It must be the talk of some regulars, though he imagined none of them were speaking in outright malice. Just intrigue. Now that Paul had come downstairs, he'd worked evenings again and was privy to the babble.

"Nothing strange about us meeting, or about him coming with David. Business doesn't stop because Christ was born, does it?" If he had been anyone else, Tom wagered Paul might laugh. He possessed dry humor, the quick kind that generally went unnoticed unless he was in company who had a similar frame of mind and keen wits.

Most people didn't.

Paul did not laugh at the mildly sacrilegious quip, though his mouth turned up a bit before he spoke. That was the slightest of victories, but it was a victory nonetheless. "You need to be careful. I do worry for you, you know. I don't know if it's wise to dally with someone associated with Mr. Mills."

"Why wouldn't it be? He's no threat to us. They're not publicans or innkeepers. Not landlords or proprietors. They trade in cloth. Have done for years, haven't they? I did hear from Rob that David is thinking of ways to venture into other industries, but I've no idea if that's true or not." Tom took a breath. "And I'm not dallying. Walking through town with a man doesn't signify anything."

"It isn't that. I'm not concerned about angering any competition," said Paul. "I also try to turn a blind eye to your affairs. It's not my place to interrogate them. But he's possessive, isn't he?" He tilted his head, and a wealth of questions were in his eyes. Tom had not told him much about what happened between him and David, and specifically avoided speaking on how they'd imploded.

He could infer that Mrs. Lloyd had heard some of the tale and possibly relayed it out of concern. If Mother or Father had known, they most likely had not spoken of it to Paul, but he doubted they'd heard anything. There were shared circles between here and Norwich, but one had to be active between them to reap the benefits of collective gossip.

"Not particularly."

"You were familiar, were you not?"

Yes. "For a short while." *Off and on for a couple of years.* "We were very silly." *We were just young.* Hell, he was still young or in his prime by most measures. He just knew more, now.

"But *you* ended things."

Not exactly.

David had suggested they continued to meet in private, or even more in private, but Tom wasn't convinced they could manage the level of deception necessary to evade Mr. Mills, who'd made it clear that Tom was no longer to go anywhere near his son, who was far too good for anything he'd indulged in.

And he was meant for better things.

Gradually, but less gradually than Tom's inexperienced heart would have liked, even if he did not believe he should have a longer time with David, David started to sound more like his father. About six weeks after the initial discussion in which Tom said they should part ways, they met furtively and David had said, "You know, Father is right about you. You *do* have an uncanny air. I don't blame myself at all."

That had been that.

Well, before that, there'd been a conversation demeaning The Shuck. David snarled he wished he could curse it, only it seemed cursed already, so why should he bother trying?

Calling a halt to all of these useless thoughts, Tom said, "His father ended things."

Paul took a few moments, possibly reflecting on what that implied. Tom allowed the quiet to blossom. Then Paul replied, "I'm sorry."

Something between them shifted, only Tom did not know what exactly, or how it moved, and he felt he would still need to tread lightly. Paul did not generally change course. He had never admitted a mistake, not even to Father or Mother, so he wouldn't take it well if

Tom pressed him. Or acknowledged his concern too much.

With a shrug, Tom said, "To answer your question, he was lost. The *dandified* secretary was lost. I helped him find his way back." That was innocuous enough.

"How do you know each other?"

"He's come to the taproom." It wasn't a lie. "I think he's called Mr. Harper. Theo Harper." Neither was that, though his use of Theo's given name didn't really speak of a proper association. *Just a haphazard one at best,* he thought, waiting for Paul to say it himself.

He didn't, not quite. "The way David used to come to the taproom?"

"No. Not all of us wish to end up like you. I wouldn't chance such a thing with someone else." Tom swallowed after he said it, knowing he should not have. Here they were, having their first true conversation in days, and he went directly for Paul's throat. His assertion, though, was really only half a truth at best.

He was grasping that he *would* hazard something with Theo if given the opportunity, which he wasn't sure would come even if he could dream. First, he'd assumed his mind was addled from his dip into the sea and the potent experience of being rescued by a mysterious man with clever brown eyes and, he wagered, more than a few secrets to keep. Their discussion in the lanes had told him as much.

In addition, he always ricocheted up after falling down, and his attempt to drown marked one such low. If he was coming up, again, he did not want to take any romantic or carnal thoughts too seriously.

His problem was exactly that the thoughts *were* serious, rambling beyond a bed and what they might do in it, and much closer to what they could do as proprietors of a business or trade.

He'd always wanted to keep a cat and wondered if Theo liked cats.

He'd been thinking of what colors they could repaint the walls and if perhaps they might get some plants suitable for indoors.

Theo would have decent opinions on both, he'd wager. His clothes were impeccable and fit him perfectly, suggesting he had a good sense of aesthetics.

Tom knew he was finally resigning himself to the idea of being bound to The Shuck, and so he wondered how it might be to have Theo keep the books and live with him in Paul's old rooms when they were cleared of the dust.

These were all dangerously outlandish thoughts.

"Well, good." Paul's lack of fight took him aback and he stared at his uncle, who lingered like a wraith. "It wouldn't do. People are fickle."

He truly must be concerned for me, thought Tom. Better tardy than never, as Mrs. Lloyd usually remarked when the groceries arrived several hours late.

At a loss, Tom said, "They can be. I don't know if they always are."

A moment of pause settled between them. Paul's defined jaw worked once or twice and it appeared he wished to say more, but could not find the right phrases to do so. Tom saw him swallow words before they formed. Then, finally, he shook his head and took his leave. When his footsteps had retreated and he had ventured to the ground floor, Tom picked up his book of fairy tales. None of them had the information he sought, though.

He wanted to find more on the story Theo had told him, the one that left him delighted he'd elected a longer route back to a path Theo knew. Not that it was a full story in the actual sense of the category. It was more of an anecdote that filled him with more queries than he could ask without extending their walk for miles. But surely it wouldn't have seemed customary to pass along the promenade more than once, and he couldn't plead ignorance to a man who he'd just gently pestered about having no sense of direction.

"When I was a child," Theo had said, turning his coat collar up against the wind, "my father said some seals were people who'd died in the sea. And they'd get one night a month—or according to some stories, one night a year—to be human again. They could come to shore on those nights, shedding their skins." Theo chuckled. "To be like the crowd."

"Is that good?" But Tom knew it could be. He'd been wondering how it must feel to be like the crowd for an age.

"Divine normalcy?" said Theo. "I think so."

Tom had heard all manner of tales from his fellow sailors and fishermen. This was a new variation on some things he'd been told with a smirk or an awed smile, depending upon who relayed the story. Oddly, more of those he'd worked with felt strongly that mermaids were real, not selkies. Most agreed those were nonsense.

Not that anyone had seen a mermaid. His thought on the entire debate was, he'd seen many, many seals, but never one person whose bottom half was a fish. The rationale of the latter made very little sense to him, whereas the prior could be feasible.

The bit about a selkie having died in the sea while still a more usual variety of person was foreign to his knowledge. But then, perhaps no sailors wanted to die just to be bound to the thing that had killed them. As he often did, Tom felt differently. Being a seal sounded restful.

"So, if I had died, some people believe I'd have become a seal?" He grinned. "Seems like a better life than this one. Simpler, anyway."

Theo paused. Apart from the somber topic, Tom couldn't guess why he looked so pensive. "I suppose it could be simpler. I don't know about better," said Theo.

They walked for a few companionable moments before he spoke again. "Part of the story, any selkie story, as I'm sure you know. . ."

"Take their skin, and you've got yourself a selkie for the rest of your life. Yes, that part always comes up," said Tom, glancing at the sky as it started to drop cold rain that would have become ice under other conditions. It would not linger, but it was still bitter. He quickened his footsteps. He continued, "Which doesn't surprise me at all. Men are often covetous. Perhaps more often than that, they're scared."

"Of what?" said Theo.

"Being left? Disloyalty? Being proven wrong? Looking the fool? Take your pick." Skin-stealing was supposedly the most attractive aspect of the whole affair. On the whole, it had been the most alluring prospect for many of Tom's acquaintances. It seemed that if they did not seek the company of their own sex, they were quite taken with the thought of a woman who could not leave. This was a convenient test for determining who he could stand being friends with.

Even some of those whom he knew were interested in men still expressed interest in a wife who could never stray.

"Yes, I rather think people are often petrified."

"They always struck me as sad," said Tom, "those selkie myths."

"Really?"

"Oh, yes," said Tom. "What right would we have to steal something so important? It's never taken with consent, not in the stories I've been told, at any rate. That's horrid. Gives awful meaning to taking a wife, doesn't it?" When Tom looked at Theo with a smile, he wasn't prepared to see the shock on Theo's face. The tip of his nose and his cheeks were rosy, the pink blooming against his tan. "What is it? What's wrong?"

"Nothing. I've just never heard someone say so."

"I'm not expressing the popular sentiment. I know," said Tom. "But it's not the same as, oh, Prometheus stealing fire for all of humanity, is it?"

"How on earth did we get to Prometheus?" Theo said, but he seemed amused. Tom could detect no antagonism. It was so blasted easy to speak to him.

"You're not helping anyone with that kind of stealing. You'd be depriving someone of their choice. Their life. Her life. Most of the time, they're women, aren't they?" He was not uneasy as he spoke, but he'd never voiced these opinions to another person and had to remind himself to stay succinct. He knew spouting such things would make him sound like a radical. "I am sorry. I suppose I shouldn't take so much from a folktale."

"Don't apologize. And it's what myths are for, isn't it?"

"Inspiring sentiment for creatures who don't exist?"

"Well, there are more things in heaven and earth, and all that," said Theo. His eyes were warm. "But they're for inspiring feeling, I should think. Making one think about things. It's not just about passing the time, though there's always room for a good bedtime story."

"God, I read fairy tales before bed and hide the books."

Sizing him up through the rain, Theo only said, with the barest hint of irony, "It's a bit at odds with your age."

"And my demeanor."

"Yes, but the contrast is wonderful. It's whimsical. Keeps me on my toes. I like whimsy."

If you like whimsy, Tom had wanted to ask, *why the hell are you with David?* The least whimsical person in the county, country, and possibly upon the earth.

The whole conversation just added to the growing fascination he had with Theo. He'd revisited it frequently.

His singular opinions about liberty and selkies seemed to touch him, which was the most perplexing aspect of all. Tom had learned through painful experience, mostly from David and a few far more innocent childhood friends, that tenderness was something to be derided. He never could integrate the lesson the way David seemed to and it still loomed whenever he expressed softness only to fear he'd be disdained.

Mostly, what he'd learned was to be gruff and to withhold his true thoughts, not to be less tender.

Yet Theo, for all Tom did not know about him, seemed content for softness to exist amongst everything else, not in contradiction of other things, but alongside them.

He did crave such a companion.

15

D avid considered himself thorough and clever, and prided himself on how Theo did not suspect he'd been rifling through the personal effects he'd brought with him for their holiday.

"That was a terrible move, David." Theo smiled as he eyed the chessboard between them.

Candlelight played on Theo's face as David watched him across the table, and it gave his skin a warmth that gaslight and especially electric light, useful as they both were, couldn't match. They did not usually dress for dinner when they were alone. Though David did love to see him in his best attire, something about less formal clothes suited him better than finery.

He reasoned they had to be what Theo preferred for himself because his demeanor changed for the better when he wore things at his leisure. David noted he seemed to favor things that were well-worn and well-loved, despite being an unfair epitome of beauty who could dress to put anyone to shame. *There can't be another reason for that odd fur to be in the bottom of his portmanteau.* One would have to prefer the rustic to the refined to carry it around and Theo always did. It had to be related to sartorial preference or sentiment.

Indeed, he carried himself more confidently in these trousers and this brown smoking jacket than he ever did in a suit. It was a shame, because he was stunning. He was magnetic and tended to draw people to him, something that David liked or was threatened by, depending on the hour.

"Yet you still play with me." David, who had never pretended to be good at chess and was actually ambivalent to it as a game, chuckled.

"It's great fun to win."

In a way, David envied his ease with chess and sartorial matters. He believed clothes were his battle armor and always felt a bit raw when he dressed for leisure and not power, but then, perhaps it was because he'd come from cloth merchants. It might be in his blood. "How fun can it be when your adversary is so awful? Must be like playing with a child."

"Oh, playing with children is fun. Even if the children are bad-tempered."

"I do hope you aren't likening me to a *bad-tempered* child."

Arch in his response, Theo said, "Never. I will say, though, there's something satisfying about teaching a child how to play a game like chess."

It was strange to David that Theo had considered it. He didn't think he'd actually done it or had children of his own. He knew there were some who preferred, well, everyone, and possibly Theo was one such man. They'd never discussed it. Then again, David knew he'd only thought of children himself because his family had a business and property to pass down, not because he especially wanted them or usually found himself in the circumstances that could lead to them.

Uncomfortable, he shifted in his chair. He didn't want to think about it, but his and Theo's situation couldn't possibly be his final state. Without children, there would be no one to inherit all his grandfather and father had built. Father's voice was in his ear, clearer than if he'd been in the room.

Love doesn't come into it, David.

"I know you only play with me because I like it," said Theo, smiling at him. He added, "And because your disdain for chess is a rebellion against your father."

While David did not mind being teased about it, he had to disregard the memories summoned by Theo's playful words. Father had not been prone to showing a temper unless he was under special duress, so generally he was cold when displeased. He withheld praise and encouragement, too, but that was because he withheld nearly everything.

His lack of voiced criticism was almost more difficult than his propensity for neglecting to give kind words when they were due. The latter was common, especially among men and many fathers, and it was navigable.

Until a spectacularly foolhardy afternoon led him to a certain discovery, anyway. Then he spoke up.

That had been quite the uproar, with Father insisting the young Apollyon must have led his son astray, then deciding that David must have learned strange ways at Cambridge, *then* finally concluding that evening—when Mother convinced him to calm himself and not blame the education, which she'd always felt was the way for David to make his mark on the world—David just made a bad choice.

Tom was condemned, which was simple enough because he was a quiet and odd fellow, intense and not given to many words. He was never to come to the house again and should David happen to see him in Norwich, he was to look the other way.

Punishment came down on David's head, too. He was no longer welcome in the Cromer house either when the family resided in it or on his own, although Mother had tried to ensure this proclamation wouldn't stick. She was from Overstrand and loved their visits to the seaside. The house they'd just purchased in Norwich often left her feeling landlocked, though it had an excellent view of Chapelfield Gardens.

It was only when Father's mind faltered that he relented, and as though nothing shocking had happened, a larger bedroom that his mother had once used then became David's. The smaller one he'd used in his younger years was still empty of a bed, far more a comfortable little study than a place for sleeping. The amount of forgiveness that occurred because Father forgot, or no longer knew what he'd known, was astounding. If David hadn't experienced the events himself, he wouldn't have believed that at one time he'd been forbidden from setting foot inside this house with its views of the ocean.

It wasn't correct to say he never thought of Tom.

He thought of him often and attributed it to the lack of closure in their situation and the way it had been violently terminated. Nothing else could be appropriate, he told himself. Tom was not the sort of man with whom he wanted to associate. He could not actually lament what they might have had.

But here, at this time of the year, thinking about him was all but inevitable and it made David peevish.

He forced himself to pull himself out of his brooding and say something.

"Father was too fond of it. He was certainly the sort of man who felt winning signified brilliance. I never took to it, so it made more sense not to care so much. He would have done very well for himself at Cambridge if he wasn't pious. It was full of men who worshipped chess more than God."

"I worry with this kind of talk that his specter shall float down through the ceiling and scold us."

Wryly, David said, "If he was going to do so, he would have done it days ago, believe you me."

"I wouldn't want to tempt it, but I suppose you're right."

David frowned, then, thinking he might be wrong about what kind of ghost his father would be. He and Theo had done all manner of things worth remarking upon, but even if he were here, Father might not know what they were. "On the other hand, he wasn't compos mentis in the end. If ghosts are us as we've died, maybe he wouldn't do anything at all."

Theo blinked, the light refracting in his eyes and illuminating proper regret. For all his self-confidence and panache, Theo was always empathetic. Not for the first time, David felt guilty he had rifled through possessions that weren't his. But he couldn't apologize for something he knew was invasive, for to do so would mean admitting fault. Perhaps he would try another tactic. Honesty.

It wasn't really the Mills family way, but it might help. He could manage honesty of a sort. He stopped fidgeting with his pawn and set it down.

"I have something I want to ask."

"Yes?" Theo sat back in his chair and reached for the pipe he favored in the evenings. "If it's about Mrs. Plunkett in Ely, her son sent a note saying she's become more absentminded of late and forgot to send payment. We received it before we left to come here, actually."

"Oh, no, I haven't given her a thought for a fortnight." A jolly woman with a fondness for russet shades, she was a seamstress who often made large orders to cater to her clients who paid for her creations and alterations. He'd noticed her handwriting growing more shaky, but hadn't worried she was so far gone that she was unreliable. "I noticed you were wearing a new necklace."

Fingers moving gracefully to pack his pipe, Theo paused. Then he completed the short procedure. David wasn't keen on letting him smoke it in public, for he was neither a worker nor an old sea dog. Pipes felt démodé to David. Still, Theo looked wonderfully salt-of-the-earth smoking one.

He was, David knew, gathering his thoughts and deciding on the best way to deliver them. When they'd first met, he'd been impressed by his ability to cultivate judicious speech. At this very moment, it just irritated him.

"I'm not wearing it at present," Theo said.

"No, I had noticed that, too." Rather than ask where Theo had found it, he chose to be direct. "Did Mr. Apollyon give it to you?"

"That's your question?"

"Among others."

Before he answered, Theo lit his pipe and exhaled rich smoke. "Yes."

Inwardly, David flinched. "In what context?"

That medal had been incredibly special to someone who otherwise didn't seem to want ornamentation. Of everyone, his grandmother was, Tom said, the only person who understood him. A gift from her was meaningful in his eyes. He moved through the world like a constant outsider, whether or not he truly was one, and he could be unsettling and rarely did the done thing. David could see how a relative who believed in him would be hard to come by. His uncle, though evidently more like Tom and David wasn't a warm source of support or encouragement.

Mother had not said much after Father delivered his edicts about David being barred from the Cromer house and ceasing all association with the younger Mr. Apollyon. But she did say something to the effect of the apple not falling far from the tree.

Though he'd been shaken to bits, trying to adjust to his father's reaction and the fact he now knew his most intimate secret, he'd been able to deduce Mother meant Mr. Paul Apollyon had something in common with *him*. They'd grown up having some of the same acquaintances, so she must have known something about it. Everybody talked, much like everyone could observe and make inferences that led to the talk.

David glanced at Theo's neck, where the medal wasn't. He hadn't found it among Theo's things, either. Perhaps it was in a pocket.

Tom wouldn't have given it away for just anything. *But I never wore it.*

"I don't see any harm in telling you, David, but you must be discreet." Theo leaned toward him, beseeching.

"I hardly speak to the man and we now live in completely different places except for small portions of the year. I don't know how I'd give anything away." David tried for a scoff, though it was painfully clear to him, anyway, that his heart was not past Tom. Or perhaps not Tom, but the fledgling relationship that had been ended without his agreement.

"Well, I shouldn't think he'd enjoy you knowing what I'm about to tell you."

With a long sigh, David shook his head and took out his cigarette case. "You make it sound as though he's my sworn enemy."

"No, of course he isn't," said Theo, "but *a history* doesn't always help, does it?"

David merely glowered as he lit his cigarette. It didn't. He disliked feeling as though he was still connected to Tom by some thread of fate or fancy that seemed midnight blue to his mind's eye. It had been there since they'd met, twined around Tom's wrists and his own, and David attributed it to an overactive imagination.

"I helped him out of the water the night I came in wet."

"And he gave you his grandmother's medal?" said David.

"He did. As you see."

Nicotine might agitate him because it often did, not that he would admit such a thing to practically anyone. But he had to be doing something during this conversation or he might well be agitated anyway. It was difficult enough not to be insulted at the hand of fate—David, mostly in spite of his father, did not actively believe in God—who'd decided his first love and his current one would meet in such a situation.

It was straight out of a play. He could already guess Tom hadn't just lost his footing and been dragged under. The man had been on one boat or another for years. If he'd gone in, he'd fully meant to do so and Theo had impeded that desire.

"You stopped him from drowning."

Theo took his turn with a sigh. "I couldn't have let him die."

I couldn't have, either, was shadowed by, *How on earth did you manage that?*

Theo had only ever presented himself as a book-keeper, a secretary — someone who excelled at the mundane and exacting tasks required by men in offices, banks, or firms. He'd never mentioned being fond of swimming, much less being able to dive into winter seas and emerge unscathed at night, lugging another man who was heavier back to shore. Even those who manned the lifeboats could have trouble saving people.

With so many fishermen and so much industry focused on the water, there were men whose work it was to save others from drowning. Theo was the least likely candidate to succeed at the task. Or so David had thought. He peered at Theo with new interest. It wasn't complimentary, for he felt slighted and as though something had been purposefully hidden from him. Of course he had done rudimentary investigations on a new employee when Theo was first hired, and all of his references had been satisfactory.

If their association had remained strictly professional, he probably wouldn't have minded not knowing plenty of things about him.

But it all veered into the intimate rather than the professional some time ago and their situation was not the sort centered on clandestine assignations. Or even much privacy. They lived together; they did not go a day without seeing each other. Yet it was only now that Theo revealed these facets of himself.

"No," David said. "You couldn't have let him drown."

"I don't think you would have let him drown, either."

"It isn't as much about what I would allow, and more about what I could accomplish."

Wariness flickered in Theo's face for the first time in their present exchange. "I was lucky."

"Perhaps you were."

"I grew up near water, David." Theo tilted his head and tried to school his nervousness away, and he was good at hiding it, but David had observed so many of his moods that he knew he had not imagined it. "My father insisted I be well-prepared. I may be better situated than some others to fish someone out, but it was still luck."

"Especially in the cold."

"Yes, especially in the cold." For the first time since they had met, Theo was snappish. It was fascinating to see what it had taken to ruin his composure. Not what, but who. "He gave me the medal. In thanks, I'd assume. I don't know if he was fully aware of his actions, though, and I did plan on giving it back to him when he was well. I'm sorry if something about the exchange has offended you."

It might have been David's mistake to assume and it certainly was his misfortune, but he hadn't recognized his folly until now. Obviously, what Theo felt for him wasn't as intense as whatever he now felt for someone he'd met only days prior. "Is that why you went to his uncle's pub?"

Minute hesitation gave away Theo's falsehood. "Yes, I wanted to return it."

"But you didn't."

"No, I didn't. There wasn't the opportunity. I didn't want to discomfort him while he was supposed to be working." Theo spoke quickly, a rapid quality to his tone that David hadn't heard previously. Then, without warning, he rose from the wide table. His movement jostled the chessboard and knocked the candlesticks, sending their flames guttering in the breeze as they remained upright. "If you'll excuse me, I think I shall—"

"Take a walk?"

Theo took the pipe from his mouth and looked at David, incredulity written on his features. "You're jealous."

"Of Tom?" David tried to infuse the two words with disdain, for he wished dearly that he was neither jealous nor suspicious. "As though I would waste time being envious of a fisherman whose uncle wants him to take over a pub with some rooms that will likely be shut within the next year. It's certainly no Cliftonville, Theo."

"Spoken like a man who is not at all jealous."

"There's no need to be snide."

David saw how other venues could draw patrons for years to come, but it was hard to understand how Mr. Apollyon managed to remain in business of late. Once an amiable if fiercely private fellow who did not fawn or offer much sporting talk, he'd kept a lovely and welcoming place. Or so he recalled it from the few childhood visits, always perfunctory and with Father for some altruistic venture or other, and the visits he'd made as a younger man to see Tom.

Neither *lovely* nor *welcoming* were words he would choose to describe The Shuck now. That did make sense given its name. When he was young, it had been called something else that now escaped him, but Mr. Apollyon's man was reputedly quite taken by the Norfolk legends of the black shuck and so they'd renamed the pub despite the sinister connotations. Perhaps the incomer valued irony more than he respected folklore.

Mother had told him one of the lanes in Overstrand belonged to *the* shuck or *a* shuck, but he'd never seen the infamous creature. Then again, he was always too scared to try looking.

Slowly, Theo said, "I don't think we have a choice when we feel envy."

Denial seemed the best course. "I feel no envy at all." He let the ashes from his cigarette fall into a large seashell his mother had lacquered for the purpose when she realized she could not stop even her friends from smoking indoors. He knew, and Theo would know, he didn't tell the truth.

Theo inclined his head, a sly smile on his lips. "None?"

"Not a bit."

At that, Theo's slyness turned sharp and a little exasperated. "You know, his name isn't 'Tom'—but I'm sure, close as you were, you must have known already."

All David could do as he left the room was gaze at Theo's back, his hands folded tightly in his lap. Like the medal, Tom's name was not something he volunteered lightly.

This can't bode well for me, David thought.

Then he realized that even if fate had dealt him an ironic hand, it was unlikely that Theo could simply walk out of his life. Understandings had been reached and would make the logistics of breaking free a little delicate. Theo would need to consider not only finding new work, but securing a new living situation, and he was no apprentice or layabout who would settle for a shabby boardinghouse room.

Would he?

Well, he most assuredly was no apprentice, and neither was he a layabout. But beyond that, the only assumption David could feel comfortable making was Theo disliked anything subpar or ugly.

Regardless of what Theo could or would tolerate, David still did not feel ready to give him up. That might make him monstrous when not long before this conversation, he'd toyed with the idea.

There was no life he could imagine without marrying, and he knew Theo wouldn't enjoy being kept alongside a wife. Not alongside, in fact, but without any similar ties to David at all. Every time they'd timidly broached the subject of the future, it was clear where Theo stood and he was not amenable to the way many other men conducted their affairs together. He said it was disrespectful not only to him, but to any future fiancée or wife.

To David, it was the only way because it was what he had seen modeled by his peers, all of whom kept businesses and households. He was no proponent of free love, though he could admit it was one manner through which such complexities could be solved.

As he stared at the empty doorway and the corridor beyond, he concluded he could not abide the thought of Theo leaving him before he was ready to be left, which was irksome. He did not want to care so much.

He wouldn't do anything to harm him, of course, and if it came right down to it, well, he would have to let Theo leave. He'd never force anyone to remain with him. It just hurt far more than he wished to say that their togetherness was amounting to so little.

He pushed his chair back, stood, and went to the portmanteau where Theo kept his personal items. Seized by the need to do something in retaliation for the pain he felt, he first wondered if he could take

Tom's medal. Then he reminded himself it probably wasn't here and left unattended.

David paused with his hands on either side of the portmanteau's top. He smirked as the solution came to him.

Even if he could not find the medal, because he was quite convinced it was on Theo's person, he *could* deal with that dingy old fur that had always insulted his sensibilities.

As he found it beneath everything else, he knew it was juvenile of him to hide it, but he hastily folded it up and resolved to put it in his own armoire. It wouldn't hurt Theo to lose such a thing, and he wasn't even actually getting rid of it.

Though he expected this to resolve some of the tension that had been building since Theo revealed how he'd met—or saved—Tom, it did very little to help him. How could it?

Still, he told himself it was something.

16

M rs. Lloyd had surreptitiously handed him a bit of paper at supper, and all it said in a pretty scrawl was *Where we first met. Tonight? 2 a.m.?*

Tom wanted to stop Mrs. Lloyd and ask how Theo had given her the note because he had neither felt nor seen him. It had probably been a calculated delivery, though. That day, he had been out for several hours taking care of their accounts at the bank, then he met with one of their soap suppliers for another hour, which would have left Theo more than enough time to slip into The Shuck and leave without him being aware he'd come at all.

As he stood roughly where Theo had hauled him back to land, he admitted he could never have stayed away from this meeting for anything. Selfishly, he longed for a very specific sort of rendezvous, but the most rational part of him knew it wasn't for that at all. Whatever there was between him and Theo, it felt like it had the potential to be more difficult than a casual meeting.

He gazed at the sea, which on the night he'd tried to die felt so perfectly brutal. Now, it felt so wonderfully rhythmic. If one had to succumb to the decency of doing their family duty, keeping a pub near to the water was not so terrible.

Theo said, as his delightful sparkling impression heralded him, "I hoped you'd come. Right after I handed Mrs. Lloyd that note, I worried you might see it as insensitive."

"Why?"

"Well, thinking about what you were here to accomplish and all, I wondered if I ought to have chosen somewhere else." He came next to Tom and Tom was heartened that he stopped closer than the usual friend might.

"No, this is fine."

Theo smiled. "You don't smell like a distillery, tonight. Just Jicky."

With a chortle, Tom produced a battered flask from his coat. "Thank you very much. I've largely abstained today, but I can't entirely. If I ever wished to wean myself off, it would have to be precisely that, a weaning."

The process was not pleasant and he'd only attempted it once on his own, concluding shortly after the attempt that he'd best enlist someone else's help if he ever wished to try again. His list of candidates was short and he did not wish to distress Mrs. Lloyd. Benson would probably be of little assistance seeing as he was so fond of the stuff himself. Will might be an option, but he'd be as horrified as Mrs. Lloyd to see him in anguish.

"Oh, yes, I've seen a few of those situations." Theo frowned and did not elaborate, but he added, "So had my father."

"Still, it doesn't hurt me to cut my consumption, or

so I'm told." He took a sip from the flask, then prof-
fered it to Theo.

"Thank you."

Tom loved the energy between their fingers as he
passed the flask off. "Of course. Cold night. And I
didn't expect you had lovely things to speak about at
this hour, and here." He flipped up his collar against
the breeze and made sure his hat was secure. "Does
David know you're out?"

"Heavens, no," said Theo, after he drank. "If you
must know, I put valerian in his tea. He takes it often
enough for his nerves, so I just increased the dose. I'm
not proud of the subterfuge, but I didn't want him to
try to convince me not to go out." He took another
drink. "Once he's asleep he's immoveable, but before
then, he can be twitchy."

"What's that? The valerian?" Since Theo's father
had worked with medicines, Tom assumed it was
some kind of herb, but hadn't heard the name.

"A root. It generally helps one sleep and can calm
tensions. If he hadn't already been accustomed to
taking it, I'm sure he wouldn't have drunk anything
because it's rather bitter. I don't think anyone *likes* it,
but at least those who take it frequently understand
what it tastes like."

Tom nodded, interested to learn something new
from this precise source of knowledge. Then he said,
"Could this increased dose kill him?" Either the
humor would land or it wouldn't. Keeping his face
composed, he waited for Theo's reply.

"Sadly, no."

"What a pity." He could have watched Theo smile
all night.

But the smile was dashed as Theo seemed to think
about why he'd passed Mrs. Lloyd a note to pass to

Tom. "I'm back to Norwich tomorrow." His tongue darted between his lips to moisten the lower, and Tom pursed his own lips as though they responded to a kiss. "In confidence, I've wanted to break with David for some months, but I couldn't find the words while we were here."

"And he's rather tyrannical in his soft-spoken way."

"Yes. But. . . if you. . . when you. . . go back to the city. I know you do, sometimes. I. . . well, I don't know how long I shall be there if or when I finally succeed in leaving him." Theo shook his head. "It's not only him that's the problem, it's me. I've been complacent for too long, and I think I've lost the ability to say both 'no' and 'good-bye.'" He bussed a hand over his face. "But if you wanted to seek me out, his housekeeper is a friend of mine now and will have my address. Wherever I decide that is. David's house is an end terrace north of Chapelfield Gardens. Number eight."

Tom knew the house, though he reckoned David must have purchased it himself or his father might have a little later in life, for it was not an address David had ever alluded to.

"But before I lived with him," said Theo, "I stayed on the Earlham Road, so I think I'll go there. I do love the city, actually. Quaint place."

Though he did register the house number, Tom had stopped listening properly somewhere around *if you wanted to seek me out*. He faced Theo, smiling. "Of course I do, you mysterious fool. And of course Norwich suits you; it's full of all kinds of odd tales."

"You think I'm mysterious?"

Not, *You think I'm a fool?*

"Come now," said Tom. "How are you unaware that's how you seem?" Theo looked, indeed, like he'd never considered it. "I know next to nothing about you." That wasn't entirely true. He actually knew quite a few things about him, though they'd arrived more like springtime blooms on different trees than a tapestry that made a proper picture. Still beautiful, but not necessarily intelligible. "Well, I mean to say, I don't know it in any order." Maybe Theo didn't need to be intelligible to be a worthwhile cause, however.

"My apologies for that," Theo said, but it was given with an indulgent smile that said he was not sorry. "I suppose I just consider myself self-contained. I certainly don't try to be mysterious, although I do like the sound of it." He paused and held out his hand. Tom glanced at what it held. He couldn't entirely say why he'd offered his gran's medal in the first place, but he wasn't prepared to take it back from Theo even if it was being offered.

"Keep it."

"It's caused me no end of trouble, you know."

"Why?"

Nonetheless, Theo was already fastening it around his neck again. "David knew what it was and he was quite threatened that I had it. It put him off his chess one night."

"Never knew him to be an avid chess player."

"Oh, he's not. He does it to spite his father."

"That sounds much more like him." As Theo fumbled with the clasp, Tom said, "Let me. It's such a tiny hinge, and it's old." Carefully, deliberating over his actions before he dipped forward, Tom put his hands on Theo's. With a thrill, he smiled as Theo *let* him. "I rarely took it off, if I'm being honest, because it was so damn fussy."

"Then why did you give it to me?"

Though he'd finished securing the medal, he lingered, letting his fingers dawdle on Theo's neck.

Touching Will felt nothing like this. Nobody he'd touched felt like this. But that might be about as sensible as comparing an ember to a lit hearth. Both were pretty and had the capacity to burn, but you couldn't really warm yourself with the prior.

Tom was immensely satisfied when Theo quivered under his fingertips. When he answered him, he said quietly, "I felt compelled to. It seemed right. I don't know."

"Those first two aren't exactly meaningless, though," Theo said. "Thank you. For helping me put it back on." Like he'd had some practice at hiding it, Theo tucked it under his collar and the modest gold pendant disappeared under layers. "I do hope you call on me."

"When do you think you shall. . ."

"End things?"

"Yes." It was apparent to him anyway, that Theo was not quite willing to pursue him physically until he concluded things with David.

On a frown, Theo said, "I wonder if he will fight it. I cannot blame him, not entirely, and I don't have the heart to hurt him more than I might without meaning to."

Tenderly, Tom said, "I feel like that makes you a decent man." While all of him yearned to kiss Theo, he respected the boundaries that obliged him to wait. It was not that he had a moral issue with kissing him right this moment, for clearly some part of Theo felt underappreciated or unfulfilled, and he wanted to alleviate it. But he did not enjoy the thought of seducing a man who wished for a clean break from another.

There was too much power involved in being the one to push anything forward and he always wanted things to be as equal as they could be, anyway. His views might be different if Theo seemed less reticent, now, but he wouldn't make him any more conflicted than he already was. In this case, he wanted things to be perfect, not that any arrangement could reach perfection. But his desire dictated more of his actions than his logic, and he leaned toward Theo so that they were a scant half-inch apart.

Theo permitted it, smirking as Tom came closer. "I made an exception when you half-drowned. I won't make another one only because you're desirous." Yet when Theo closed the distance even more, narrowing the amount to a mere fraction of a half, Tom had to grasp for self-control not to finish it and kiss him deeply. He waited as Theo gently cupped his cheek. "I don't want to lie to David, you see, if he asks anything more about what we've done. I did tell him I dragged you from the water, but I don't want to have to tell him something else."

Ragged, Tom said, "That's commendable."

"I'm already lying about other things." Theo was just as taxed.

"You don't strike me as the sort who'd be happy about lies, so I am sure it's with good enough reason."

"If I didn't mind lying, I'd have you here, all the cold be damned."

"Are you positive you *do* mind?"

"I'm sorely tempted to *stop* minding, at present, if it helps." Theo stroked his cheekbone, then lower, along the edge of the stubble he should have shaved. "But I have something to tend to, first, and I can't be conflicted while I tend to it. I'll let you know when I've gone to live on Earlham Road."

"If you had me here, you're sure you'd be conflicted?" Tom did not want to coerce Theo, but he still had to say it. The very suggestion that Theo found him as compelling as he found Theo was a marvel.

With a devil's grin, Theo simply nodded.

~

THEO HAD NEVER LIKED Christmas or Hogmanay—too much fanfare and activity—but he nearly liked Christmas in Norwich. The city went remarkably cozy and charitable, and so he was almost sorry the season was now at an end.

He watched the station recede behind them before returning his attention at least nominally to David. This period immediately after the turn of the year felt like flat champagne or ale someone had left out too long, and so did their relationship as it was now.

While it was usually consumed because people felt like they had to or wanted to be drunk, it might have been better poured into the gutter. He wrinkled his nose a little, trying not to give into regret, which wasn't an emotion he often felt.

He could have made his exit before they left to return home, or to the house David called home, at any rate. It would have been so much simpler to slip away with the North Sea on his doorstep, and he could always find more things because possessions were easy to come by, so long as one was not too picky or too covetous. He had accounts with one bank in Glasgow, another in Edinburgh, and a newer one in London, so he was fortunate enough to say money posed few issues for him.

It was self-worth and self-determination that were his problems, evidently. Or, more optimistically, perhaps he *was* just growing complacent. Even more optimistically, he felt deeply for Tom and this had hindered his plans to simply go.

Some might call it sympathy for a man who distinctly felt and experienced much, but he knew himself well enough to understand what he felt was not obligation or undue compassion. Or only lust, though their meeting on the beach before he'd left had demonstrated how much there was of *that*.

"On Wednesday," said David, "I have an appointment with Mr. Tipton."

"I recall. I was the one who put it in your diary. But I thought you'd had some falling out with him," said Theo. He forced himself to look at David and smile. He'd figure a way out of his doldrums and he could change his situation without crushing David, he was certain.

While it was perturbing how David had seemed to fixate on Tom, he'd said nothing more about his former friend since the last time they'd played chess.

What he had not said, Theo had made up for by thinking of the man.

Innocent things, mostly—he wanted to take more walks, talk more, tease more. If it happened to lead to anything else, well, then that would be fully welcome. But more sensual thoughts crossed his mind, too. The point, however, was he didn't intend to seek out *anything else* until he'd concluded whatever this was.

Theo could not comprehend why David was so warm over the matter. He wouldn't have thought it was so very suspicious a man had saved another from drowning in a town bordering the sea, particularly one known for its lifeboats and fishing. Surely, even if luck had some bearing on who lived and who drowned, it was not unheard of for someone to be lucky.

"Ah, that was his father," said David. "The younger one is not so stubborn and far less likely to throw things at me."

They rattled along in their hired coach and all manner of pedestrians and conveyances were coming to life now that most winter festivities had passed. While it was unlike anywhere he'd lived and seemed to be unlike many other places in general, for many quips about Norfolk abounded in other parts of the country, he was quite at home here. It would be a shame to leave it, but he supposed he could always return to visit.

As Tom had said, David was not omnipotent. He could not be everywhere at once and he didn't own the city. Besides, they were adults and it would be ridiculous to hold onto a relationship that hadn't lasted, particularly when that relationship wasn't valid under the law and had to be hidden so much of the time.

"Oh, yes. . . you're right, it *was* his son who threw the inkwell at your head when you said the weaver had stopped producing that particular herringbone." If one believed Mr. Tipton, senior, the exact herringbone at stake was his granny and great-aunt's favorite and therefore it was inherently impertinent to suggest they should amend their habits or tastes.

When it was regretfully intimated that they might have to, pandemonium broke free.

Theo tried to intercede from across the office and was unable to stop the man from creating an extempore shell from an inkstand, so he just had to stand and watch with dread. He was greatly relieved when the poor inkstand sailed past David's head to clatter against the wall and drop sadly to the floor. There wasn't the explosive denouement Mr. Tipton had been expecting.

Not if he'd not expected to hit David's head, anyway. It was hard to say if Mr. Tipton meant to cause more of an injury or a mess.

Theo could sympathize with the prior, because at times he also wished to send something hurtling toward David's head and never chose such violence. Conversely, he did not enjoy messes.

The next day, Mr. Tipton the younger had visited to apologize and make explanations for his father's behavior. David, who was usually quite gracious when it came to business, took it well. The father did frequent them occasionally, but it was generally in the company of his son, who, now that Theo thought about it, still never allowed him near any of the stationery. Neither did his daughter, who was his younger child. She frequented the office far less often than her brother, but had accompanied either Mr. Tipton on occasion.

As he thought about these mundane occurrences, it was peculiar to realize he was used to life as it was, but had been hungering after life as it wasn't, and would soon have the opportunity to seize the latter.

Tom came to mind yet again and Theo had to ignore him, or risk certain telltale physical signs that he was thinking rather unholy thoughts.

He glanced at an especially fine horse as it passed the window of their carriage, the sun shading its tail a warm black. They would be home soon, and he could make his plans somewhere quiet.

~

WITHOUT A HINT OF IRONY, Paul set a nondescript copy of Hans Christian Andersen's tales on the table. Tom looked at him, then the book, then at him again.

"It's for you," said Paul.

"Why?"

"I missed your birthday."

"I wasn't here, anyway. Why not wait until April, then?"

"If you don't want it, don't take it."

Tom decided Paul was in earnest and trying, in his way, to be kind. "I didn't say I don't want to keep the book. . ." he shook his head. "Thank you."

"I've had it for a while, as you might be able to tell. Still, it's not so old," said Paul. The more Tom studied it, the better he could see the fine layer of dirt almost embedded into its embossed cloth binding. "But frankly, I find his stories too sad."

There was no possible way to determine what to address first: Paul read fairy stories or Paul believed something was too sad. He'd never been seen with a book of fiction, or at least, Tom hadn't noticed him with one. While he had emotions, clearly, for no man without an excess of emotion would lead his life as Paul did year after year, one would be quite pressed to decipher how he actually felt about a lot of things.

Tom thought that was on purpose, for a curmudgeon could feel whatever he wanted and no one would know on account of him being so unpleasant to deal with. He wouldn't be bothered by either well-wishers or detractors. It was rather a dangerous game to play when there was an abundance of inns and public houses in not only Cromer but any other nearby town, village, or city, but they'd never exactly suffered and watching him with his customers was like watching another person control his body.

"I just thought you just believed fairy tales were worthless."

"I worried they might predispose you to believe things that weren't possible."

"I think that's the point of them, is it not?"

Unless, and this was most likely what Paul worried, he referred to the everyday things one could extrapolate from folklore. That there could be happiness, that love existed, that there might be the chance to wander and find the extraordinary, that there would be danger but it could be faced and surmounted. On the other hand, the stories Tom often enjoyed didn't have what he'd term a happily ever after, or if there was one, it came with caveats and complications. Sometimes ones that couldn't be magically resolved.

Yet, their endings were frequently the sweetest. Perhaps Paul meant those.

His mind drifted to the beach where he and Theo had last spoken.

"Yes, well. Careful not to become too carried away," said Paul. "I need you here."

Is he dying? It was the least decent question one could ask of possibly anyone at all, and hardly the sort of question Tom would ask an uncle who—with the exception of the most recent period of time—had not seemed keen to speak to him about anything deeper than the right kind of floor polish.

They were alone but for Benson, who kept flitting in and out of the taproom like a human-sized butterfly trying to escape a determined scientist who was intent upon capturing him. Still, Tom would refrain from asking the offensive and obvious.

But his thoughts must have been on his face.

"I'm not infirm. Well, I'm not any more infirm than

I was before I rejoined the world of the living." Paul's voice did not give any arch humor away, but his eyes were smiling, which was both comforting and some-thing Tom hadn't seen in ages. What Paul said next would have had him finding a chair, had he been standing. "I wish to repent for the years I've spent dis-daining you purely because I also disdained me."

While Tom deeply wanted to be the sort of man who said no, held grudges, and protested that the time for apologizing or repenting would have been during his formative years when he'd needed more protection and understanding, he wasn't. He also wanted to be skeptical.

He wasn't.

Paul had always shown glimpses of warmth and was always decent, it was just that neither of those qualities had normally been directed at him. He'd seen it in the way he'd dealt with drunk customers, patrons who couldn't quite pay for their room and board in full, Mrs. Lloyd after Mr. Lloyd passed, and Mother after Father passed. All things considered, he was quite tender.

"You don't need to repent," said Tom, "but I will take any books you don't enjoy off your hands."

"You don't want to see how neglected they've been."

"There are many reasons I don't want to see how you've been keeping yourself, but the books aren't one of them. Anyway, I'm no librarian."

Tom sat back on the bench, an old wooden thing that looked almost like a church pew. It might have been, for who knew what had been dragged into The Shuck by any proprietors whose pragmatism out-weighed their sense of decorum or superstition. He surveyed Paul with a renewed sense of empathy, one he felt he could more openly display even though they had not spoken of much at all. The feeling between them had changed, not just in the way only Tom could sense—so far as he knew, anyway—but in the more earthy, mundane manner shared by anyone.

"Don't," said Paul gently. "You don't need to feel sorry for me. Indeed, you shouldn't. I've behaved abominably." He smiled. "Don't tell your mother, whatever you do. I'll never hear the end of it if she finds out I've finally admitted to you how terrible I've been. And make no mistake, I have been. My intention in being so unapproachable does not matter."

"I haven't yet been to visit her, and I don't write to her nearly as much as I should. She shall not hear anything from me."

"Not even over Christmas?"

It was Tom's turn to be gentle. "I thought it was better to stay here while you weren't engaging with anything."

"I can rouse myself if someone needs a bed." Paul smiled. "I'm less apt to do so if they need a drink. Those who want one always seem to be able to find what they need well before I make it downstairs to serve them." The smile blossomed into a proper grin. "How do you think I've kept this place so many years? Can't have turned everyone against me, can I?"

"I'll admit, it was slightly mystifying."

Somber, eyes on the whitewashed wall behind Tom's head, Paul heaved a sigh as though he were letting out years' worth of tension. "I realized what you had ahead of you, and I. . . instead of perhaps taking you under my wing, properly. . ."

Tom could have said a number of spiteful things. He tried to choose grace while his mind caught up to the mirage before him. "Paul, it's all past, isn't it?"

As he reflected, he began to suspect the seeds for this apology were better rooted than a copy of Andersen's stories. Had his father still been alive, it would have been simpler for him to take over more responsibilities at the pub his mother and stepfather now oversaw. Although no one would have protested had his mother taken her dead husband's role—there was so much precedent—her new husband did not deem it proper. They did work together to manage the pub, but he was not interested in Tom's help.

Mother had believed she was remarrying for love. Tom believed it, too, because she had no need to marry at all. She'd inherited the business from his father, after all, and would have both an income and home of own. Her son was grown. A husband wasn't necessary for material reasons as he might be for other widows.

But after remarrying, it became clear that even if her new husband had married for love, too, he had strict ideas on what his wife should be doing with herself. It was ludicrous, seeing as when they met she was already acting as proprietor and Tom had been performing much the same duties he did now under Paul's direction.

It was only after she'd taken a new husband that it became clear Tom, even having been raised to know all manner of things to do with innkeeping and public houses and hospitality in general, was no longer welcome. Mr. Peel's flimsy reason for barring him was that he'd previously chosen another trade entirely.

If, maintained Peel, he'd intended upon being a proprietor or landlord all along, he should not have wandered off and taken up with fishermen, dockworkers, or *their ilk*.

Mother had pointed out they served fishermen, of

course, and she wanted to know what was wrong with them or anybody who took up a trade that only put food on people's tables. And them on the docks, she said, did equally important work.

It hadn't worked, for the response was just more questioning of Tom's ability to devote himself to something. That wasn't a fair assumption, as he'd been on boats since the time David was in his second year at Cambridge and around the docks before that. He'd only come back to help Mother when she sent word Father was ill, and Father passed not long after he returned. Then she remarried about half a year later.

He could commit to a trade, but evidently it was not the correct one and it undid any training he'd received as a boy. In the end, it was probably most accurate to say his stepfather instigated his relocation to The Shuck. He'd insisted Tom was no longer welcome or needed, so Mother prevailed upon Paul. It only occurred to Tom at this moment that by helping her—no, *him*, really—Paul might have been trying in his imperfect and remote way to begin to make amends.

"I. . . yes, it is," said Paul. "But I am not proud of how I behaved."

He'd focused more of his ire on Paul, but he should have turned it to Mr. Peel. "I think if you were trying to prevent me from becoming more like you, you failed."

"If that was what I was doing, there was little excuse for how I went about it. How were you to know I was worried?"

"Can I ask. . ." Tom chewed at his lip, then just came out with it. "Why. . . is this time every year so. . . difficult?"

"Come. You must know. Mrs. Lloyd must have said."

"Well, I know what she surmises." Tom grimaced. "But I don't know if it's true."

Taking his time to respond, Paul said at length, "I don't feel ready to talk about it. But I will tell you, if you ever wondered, Alistair and I were..."

Tom could fill the pause with the words he thought Paul might be reviewing in his mind. *Together. In love. Besotted. Happy. Married in all but name.*

He couldn't claim to have known Alistair well, especially because he was not here throughout the year to spend much time with the two of them. But his wraithlike mark was gold, and suggested pine needles, and always carried a little of Paul's birch tar. That mutual, slight blending happened only with affectionate couples who came to The Shuck or anyone whom he knew to be in a happy arrangement, and prompted Tom to assume they were a pair before he had proper language for the thought.

Abruptly, he realized it hadn't happened between David and Theo.

David was still resolutely himself, earthy loam and something piquant and green like absinthe, and that hadn't changed since they were boys.

Well, it boded well for *him* that they hadn't reached that point, although he did not want to be too smug about it.

"Companions," was what Paul ended up saying. There was such a wealth of meaning in the single word that Tom wanted to embrace his uncle for the first time in years. But because he did not want to shatter their present entente, he remained on the old pew and just let Paul take his time speaking. The fire crackled and a wall settled.

With a nod, Tom said, "I thought so. I didn't tell anyone."

Dismissively, Paul said, "You would be surprised how many people know and how many don't actually mind as long as you're not getting in their way with it. I take comfort in the idea that I'm neither important nor wealthy, so really, there's nothing anyone could want out of me enough to cause trouble."

"And you're not going after boys," said Tom. No adult he'd kept company with had ever done such a cruel thing.

"Lord, no. I'd gut anyone like a fish if I knew they'd done it." He grinned. "Alistair did, once, or so he said. He liked to tell tales, so I'm not certain if he truly did so or just bloodied someone's nose to make his point." The expression that followed Paul's words and his smile was so pensive it almost hurt to see it, and the emotions behind it weren't even his to bear.

"Are you certain you don't wish to talk about it?"

Paul looked at the backs of his hands and shook his head. "I don't know what there is to say. I don't want it to sound like an excuse."

"It isn't. I'm asking you what happened. I'd understand if perhaps you wouldn't want to tell a child about it, but you can speak to me now." Tom waited a few seconds. Then, tentatively, he said, "I was given to think he just left you, but I don't believe that's true."

A breath passed before Paul answered. "He didn't leave. He died."

This, more than anything, would explain his yearly seclusion. If they'd loved each other, the bereavement would have left Paul as a grieving widower in all but title. Tom kept his hands still on the top of the book. "Is he buried here?" He truly couldn't make a decent conjecture. Paul was so particular and quiet in his ways that he could have been going out to visit a grave all this time, and no one would know unless he wished them to know.

But the reply surprised him.

"No. But I don't know where they took him."

Tom didn't want his mouth to gape, and it still did. "Pardon?"

"It was complicated. He was older than me by more than a decade, a widower, and had a son who was grown. With a young family. When Alistair met me. . . well, it wasn't *supposed* to be anything at all." Paul traced a jagged scratch on the bar. "But when it became something, he tried to be as open as he dared. Of course, he didn't give details. All he ever really said was he was taking work here." He glanced at Tom and gave a tired smile. "I think James, the son, suspected his father before I was part of his life. I don't know if his mother might have said something. If she knew at all."

"If he told him that much, that he'd come here, he didn't mean to abandon him?"

"Correct. He wrote every fortnight or so, but James never replied. I didn't want to pry, so it wasn't until he died that I looked through his diary and took the address. It wouldn't have been right not to tell James."

"Of course," said Tom. He was fighting to keep up with these revelations, but understood that immediately. "Did Mother and Father know?"

Paul nodded and his smile became less tired. "They knew." He chuckled. "Your father always knew about me. Even before I finally told him. But. . . I didn't want to draw more attention to Alistair and me than we might have had already, so that was why we never went to Norwich together to visit any of you."

"Did they know he died?"

"Yes. I don't know how you escaped the knowledge

yourself, if I'm being honest, although. . ." he frowned, seeming to think back to a memory that was dulled by time, excess emotions, or both. "I never spoke to you about it. And because he didn't have a wake or a funeral here, it was a remarkably quiet affair. They came in the morning to take him, and some are tending to their business, then, but it wasn't as though the whole town was watching."

Reluctantly, Tom asked, "But you. . . really. . . don't know where they took him."

"I don't." Paul sounded as dour as he often appeared, but only for a flash. "James said he'd involve the law if I tried to interfere. I didn't want to interfere, and I didn't want to keep him from his father. I never wanted that. I only wanted to. . ." he quieted and inhaled. "I only wanted to know where he was going."

It was just a vague threat, but it was menacing enough that it held weight. Paul had a livelihood to consider, not a famous name or any kind of wealth. While tarnishing the latter two in court would likely lead to infamy and possibly a change in circumstance, losing the prior could lead to destitution.

Tom reached over and covered Paul's fidgeting hand with his. One didn't need special powers to feel his anguish, no matter how comparatively measured he was while relaying it. It would be torturous to be denied that knowledge, he felt. He wanted to be purely furious toward Alistair's son, but under his fury was a grudging understanding. He couldn't condone James, but neither could he pretend he didn't know many people would act similarly. "Thank you for telling me."

"I'm so sorry it wasn't a better example for you."

Incredulous, Tom said, "But your life isn't meant to be an example to anybody." This shame that it supposedly wasn't a good example, he understood, was probably why he'd never heard the truth from Paul himself.

But the phrase that reverberated most from his uncle's words was, *it wasn't* supposed *to be anything at all.*

A meeting with someone who wasn't supposed to be anything might become the most provoking *something.*

17

B enson didn't enjoy reading for leisure.
   So Tom had thought, until he appeared
   the next evening with a book that looked like
an old encyclopedia. It could have been fished out of
one of the college libraries of Cambridge that David's
sort enjoyed bragging about.

He eyed Benson as he puttered about, first examining a rusty stain on the hearthstones that looked suspiciously like old blood, then an ochre pillow on the chair nearest the doorway, still holding his decrepit book as he completed his inspection of things he saw daily.

Tom hadn't been convinced Benson could read very well. Even during their journeys to Norwich, Benson did not read timetables before setting off, or so much as a magazine in front of him on the train. Everything he learned, he seemed to learn from a conductor or a kindly stranger. Not that he really needed to learn anything given he was older than the hills and rarely left Norfolk.

Tom had retreated from the busy, warm taproom and the common area was drafty, so he was presently lounging on a dilapidated wingback in front of the fire and trying desperately not to think of a certain Mr. Harper with earnest brown eyes. He concentrated on the cheerful flames before him.

He knew which of the two would warm him more, not that it helped to know. It had been almost two weeks since he'd last seen him, since their mouths lingered close and teased a kiss, but their ethics prevailed over a moment's demanding feelings.

"Selkies."

Tom glanced at Benson's craggy face, then the book, which had an almost equal number of creases intersecting its spine. "Pardon?"

Benson cleared his throat, sounding not so much like a man as he did a rusted door forced to open for the first time in a decade. He really ought to see a doctor.

"Selkies," he repeated, once he had regained his breath.

Well, Tom had not thought the word and he certainly had not spoken it in Benson's presence. Nor had anyone else, most likely.

He smiled. "What about them, Benson?"

As he had intermittently during their entire acquaintance and especially of late, he momentarily wondered if Benson was sharper than he acted. He could see how shamming madness might be an advantage. After all, his own defense against unwanted interactions was grumbly solitude, just as Paul's had been toward him.

People did leave one alone if they thought ill of you, and so he imagined it would be if one was thought to be slightly or entirely odd. Then again, he did not quite know if the two were exclusive. Indeed, he could not say if he was only pretending to be a killjoy and he was—certainly, by some standards—not compos mentis.

Perhaps you just are one and you are also mad. They weren't exclusive states.

"One might call for you," said Benson.

"For me, specifically?"

Taking a seat on the matching chair opposite his, Benson shrugged, then set the heavy tome on a low table between the chairs. "Think so. Noticed anyone new underfoot, recently?"

Now, that was uncanny if it wasn't just coincidental. Tom bit his lip as he considered Benson's question. He had been dwelling rather too much on one new person who'd been underfoot, which was the entire trouble of the matter, and he exhaled.

He should put his book down. He hadn't even really been reading it, anyway; it dangled listlessly from his hand while he stared at the fire like one entranced, so he closed it and settled it on his thigh. "It's my trade to notice them. They're the ones without places of residence. It's generally why they're here."

Paul, who must have been lurking somewhere and doing something that needed to be done at this time of night, gave a dry laugh that Tom could only just catch. Benson either did not hear it, or ignored it. "It's far more subtle than any of your gothic stories could make it," he said. Benson knew Tom's habits. "Their call, I mean. It's not anything so overt."

Tom could not even bring to mind one novel using a selkie as hero or villain. "Is it?" He was nonetheless relieved not to immediately discuss Theo, who was the only newcomer he could summon from memory.

Like his mind was a compass and the man bloody due north.

"Subtler than any legends about a witch, too," said Benson.

"Who said anything about witches?" Bringing a finger to his lips, Tom tapped them to avoid smiling or giggling or looking amused in any manner. Benson despised being the focus of humor.

"I did."

"Yes, well."

"They're a kind of magic, you know."

"Witches?"

"No," said Benson. He scowled. "Of course witches are magic, just like them who detect them. Selkies, Silence, *selkies* are a kind of magic." Benson was the only person besides his uncle who ever used his proper given name. Not even Mother did it.

Half the time he did and the other half he did not, as though to remind Tom he had two names and both were viable. More likely, he just forgot which was the one Tom preferred. As a boy, it had felt mean-spirited. But when he'd told Benson to say "Tom," Benson did. Then, over time, he'd started with "Silence" again and Tom attributed it to forgetfulness.

Paul was *definitely* laughing somewhere very nearby, possibly having abandoned his task to properly eavesdrop. Tom smelled faint, spectral birch tar as well as heard the chuckling, now persuaded Benson surely could *not* hear the latter. He must not be obfuscating a full level of hearing, even if he pretended to be so bizarre. His ears really had to be dwindling and he must not hear the laughter. Tom did not think even Benson and Paul's loyal friendship would protect Paul from a scathing lecture on how a man should be taken seriously.

Though he did not wish to add to any distress, for it was not something he was inclined to do for those he liked or loved, Tom struggled to keep a composed expression. "You only just thought a cavalcade of witches was to descend on Cromer, but I have yet to see any of them. Now you're on about selkies?"

"You wouldn't notice them," Benson said. "They look just like ordinary people. Not unless you were trained to."

"Like you?"

"Yes," said Benson stoutly.

"How much gin have you had to drink?"

"Less than you."

"I don't favor gin, so that would not be difficult." It was the only spirit he didn't favor. Juniper's astringent tang didn't agree with him. Tom raised an eyebrow in a gentle, teasing rebuke. "Not only do I doubt their existence. . . I have to wonder, too, what they'd be doing here."

He was lying, because if he might believe in anything besides his own experiences of what the likes of Baudelaire might call synesthesia and others would dismiss as madness, it would be seals who were people. It wouldn't necessarily be witches or sorcerers, although given enough evidence, he'd believe in them as well. Anyway, if Benson was to be believed, all of these categories of beings were bound by magic. He breathed the tiniest of sighs.

Luckily, Benson did not take his playful reproach as a reprimand. "They might be looking for a protector, looking for a similar type of magic, looking for a friend," he said, counting each category on his gnarled fingers. Then he added, clasping his hands together and shuffling close to the fire, "Or perhaps they are only sampling a new fish. Who knows?" With an inscrutable expression, he concluded, "There are predators and there are protectors. Don't be a predator. But then, I don't think you've ever been one of those."

"I have no idea what. . ." At a loss, Tom stopped talking.

Then Benson leaned toward him and the façade finally broke. A hare's quickness was in his eyes. "Mr. Mills is in a pickle," he said, his voice barely above a mutter. "He's no predator, either, though I fear he may fancy himself one with all his father's words in his lonely head."

How a supposedly addled old man could understand how David struggled to keep a tender disposition from taking the fore was impossible to know. Tom had seen it in small ways or else they could not have been friends, he was sure of it. But the unfortunate effect of David's fight to be both more—and not at all—like his father was that he did not have his conviction, just all of the aloofness. The struggle itself had robbed him of verve.

On the other hand, Benson had been local to the area his whole life and everyone knew the deceased Mr. Mills' reputation. It might not be inordinately difficult to understand his son's predicament if one was even slightly aware of his father's behavior.

Regardless, Tom embraced Benson's lucidity and took it for what it was. He could interrogate how he felt about it later. "David is in trouble?"

Benson nodded. "I reckon he's stumbled into the middle of something he doesn't understand."

"It's that Harper fellow, isn't it?"

Tom craned his neck to gape at Paul, who'd come silently to his side and stood near his chair. He huffed. Anyone with an interest in gossip seemed to know Theo and David were—at the very least—*employer and employee*.

But he was startled because Paul could move more quietly than a cat and often did. More than once, Mrs. Lloyd had tutted about how she wanted to sew small bells into his clothes, though how she would manage to keep it a secret endeavor until she managed to do so, she didn't know.

"Surprised you could pull yourself out of your yearly lovesick stupor long enough to notice," said Benson.

It was the most direct sentence Tom had ever heard him utter. And the most lively. And the most intimate. But never mind that Paul seemed to share a secret knowledge with Benson, Tom wanted to know what they knew about Theo.

"It's a most difficult time of year, but I'm not incapacitated," Paul said. He sounded tickled. Keeping quiet, Tom wanted to know what else he had to say. "And I felt him when he came in, though I was above stairs *and* out of sorts."

Felt him? Felt who?

"Imagine how I felt when he was speaking to me," Benson said, straightening up and sitting correctly in his own chair. He grinned, revealing a couple of his handful of missing teeth. "The threads coming off him. . . poetic. Color of a deep red rose in sunshine."

"What is he, then? He's certainly not Jack Valentine," said Paul.

"Think Silence knows even if he doesn't know."

Tom scowled. Silence certainly did not know. Not why Paul mentioned Theo, or what he meant by *feeling* Theo, or what Benson meant by sunshine and roses, either. Or what David had to do with anything at all, other than he and Theo plainly had an accord. He felt more drunk listening to this exchange than he ever did after consuming an entire bottle. Paul glanced at Tom with a little pity, but he thought there was reassurance in it, too.

"Come now, Benson, don't play with us," said Paul.

"You might think we'd see more of them since we're so near the sea and all," said Benson. Of course, he played with them. "Perhaps they're just more northern creatures? I've only met two in my time. Wonderful, both of them. Mary is still with us, I do think, although the lovely Vera may have passed on, now. I was never entirely sure of her age as she was not forthright about it, and why should she be forthright about anything? Especially with a man."

"You have shown your hand already, so don't pretend to be in possession of a meandering mind now of all times," said Paul, tolerantly and with only the narrowest edge of impatience. He rested his palm on the top of the chair as though to stay Tom and keep him from rising. He underestimated Tom's desire to know what Benson was talking about.

Leaving the room would not be in his plans until he untangled what Benson meant.

The answer was already within his mind and lurking just outside his reach, Tom was certain. He could not say how he knew, as with much he knew, but he had enough familiarity with forces and qualities he couldn't see to doubt himself.

He said, "David—Mr. Mills—is in trouble because of Theo?" Paul smirked, so Tom amended, "I mean to say, Mr. Harper."

In the strictly mundane sense, it was not impossible, but Benson was not insinuating legal trouble and neither of the men in question would belie their true affections. It would cause too much trouble for both of them even if one wished to exact some kind of petty revenge or an agenda on the other. Theo seemed to value his autonomy, while Tom knew David valued his reputation. They were perhaps very different reasons and values, but both were persuasive.

"Not because of him, strictly speaking," Benson said.

"Out with it," said Paul. "No one is here to overhear us, and they're all pleasantly drunk by now. I've slipped off to dust." He winked.

"Can't you feel it?" Benson's question wasn't addressed to Tom alone, but Tom got the sense Benson wouldn't mind if he answered along with his uncle.

Heaving a sigh much like the ones Tom kept expelling, Paul shook his head. "I know something is amiss because Mr. Harper departed for Norwich, did he not?"

Before Tom could stop himself, he said, "Yes. He's gone."

Paul gestured at him as though to say, *Thank you.* "But somehow, I still expect him to walk through the door and clear through to my taproom. Beyond what I know I sense, I cannot say what it means, you impossible sorcerer."

"So you can," said Benson. "Feel his impressions."

"I may not cultivate it for my profession the way you do, but yes."

Tom had just about given up trying to divine meaning from anything they were saying when Benson switched his attention and addressed him directly. "I would wager things feel that way to you, too." Benson was correct, but predominately because Theo haunted Tom's daydreams and warmed his blood.

Then Benson contradicted that thought. "And not because he's turned your head."

Christ almighty, it appeared everyone was suddenly aware and accepting of his inclinations. "I . . ." he looked up at Paul as he unthinkingly mussed his own hair, trying to glean some clue as to how he should respond.

With a new shade of sensitivity, Paul said, "If we weren't nattering away at you and you could just be peaceful in your own mind, and close your eyes, would it feel at all like Mr. Harper might be. . . oh, standing right near me?"

"I thought that was naught but wishful thinking." Except he didn't. Not really. He'd experienced infatuations before and knew the difference between fancies and whatever kind of magnetism had drawn him to Theo.

"It is not," said Paul. Then, without any elaboration and leaving Tom's mouth partially open in consternation, he narrowed his eyes at Benson and reiterated his most pertinent question. "What is Mr. Harper? What is Vera, and what is Mary? You know I am not acquainted with them, so those references mean nothing to me."

"Very well. I never get to have this kind of fun, so you cannot blame me for dragging it out."

"Benson, please."

"What on earth do you mean, *what* is he?" asked Tom. "He's surely just a man."

"I owe you another discussion," said Paul quickly, his eyes on Benson but his words directed at Tom.

Benson steepled his fingers together and said quietly, "He's a selkie. But we mustn't go spreading it around, for that never ends well for them."

It should not have made sense.

It did. Tom had to grip both arms of his chair as though he might tumble off the edge of a cliff if he didn't grasp at something solid, but it did make sense.

"Wait. I've never met one," said Paul, and he stepped between Tom and Benson's chairs in order to speak more quietly. "So I don't understand. What has that to do with him haunting the town, for lack of a better term?"

His uncle should not be accepting 'He's a selkie' with the calmness of one declaring that they took sugar in their tea. Well, most would be calm when delivering such a declaration about tea. Someone was likely just as intense about their tea preferences as the supporters of a particular racehorse on racing day.

"He isn't. He haunts nowhere," said Benson. "But I suspect Mr. Mills has done the unthinkable."

Tom instantly intuited, perhaps not very astutely given the narrow subject, that Benson believed David had Theo's skin. But it was very thinkable if the legends held any truth. Many men had thought and done it, supposedly. He was heartened that Benson called it unthinkable, though, for he knew not many men would find it so. He thought of his peers, the ones who'd relished the thought of capturing a woman with her skin, and frowned. Without his skin, Theo would have very little freedom.

"How?" said Tom.

"The same way anyone does," said Benson. "You just take it."

"He wouldn't have told David what he was." Tom huffed when they both looked at him with rivalling expressions of incredulity. Or it could have been pride. Pride in what, he couldn't say, but he could guess they were proud of his pragmatism. Proud that he wasn't in need of smelling salts or calling for someone to incarcerate them.

Not that he would ever want anyone imprisoned for madness. It would make him a hypocrite of the highest order.

"I needn't have taken him to bed to learn that," he said in reply to their looks, throwing aside any attempts at preserving niceties or the illusion that he did not enjoy men. "It's obvious when he talks about David and their. . . whatever agreement they have. He wouldn't tell him." Mulishly, he added, "Though I've been as a man possessed since I met him, so I may not be the most unbiased person."

There. He also cast aside the pretense that he refrained from enjoying men, which he often had, but not now that he preferred a specific man. Theo was a *very* specific man, and he was discovering that this newfound, arcane knowledge about his situation —*Can I call it a situation?*—did not deter his interest.

"But you still somehow know he wouldn't tell his lover something of great import, something very strange, that *you* seem to be accepting with alacrity," said Benson, drier than autumn leaves underfoot. "Are you a bit strange yourself?"

"He didn't tell *me*, either," said Tom, finally releasing his grip on the wingback's armrests. *What if the way he brought up the legends about suicides and the sea was his way of telling you?*

If that were so, it had been too subtle of an attempt. Wherever Theo was, Tom's ability to understand and embrace nuance was not. He clouded his judgement and finer senses, mundane or otherworldly. Still, in retrospect, it did seem he was testing Tom's potential reactions to the themes themselves. It might explain why Theo was so touched by Tom's insistence that the selkie myths were sad.

"It sounds like he might have, had you spent any more time together," Benson said.

"Well, he needn't have told *him* for David to discover what he is," Paul interjected, probably before Tom could bristle.

He wasn't bristling. It was a novel and charming sensation to be agreeably teased for what he was. No, the only development that was still somewhat unbelievable or insupportable to him was Benson's lucidity, and that was quickly settling into a truth he had to accept.

"I think you give David too much credit, Benson," said Tom. "You think he stole a selkie's skin when he stopped believing in God before anyone else I knew." He shook his head. "If he has a skin in his possession and it happens to allow a man to turn into a seal, he only has it because he thinks any associate of his should never wear such a thing. He wouldn't know the truth. Theo wouldn't have told him, and even if Theo tried, he probably wouldn't believe it. Things must fit into a neat category for the Mills."

He ignored the looks Benson and Paul both gave, presumably because he'd used *Theo* twice in one sentence and it was the longest speech they'd heard from him in a long time. Years, probably.

Benson appeared mollified that his point was being made, though Tom wasn't sure which point was the most pressing or if any of them were being made at all. Paul seemed wistful as though Tom had mentioned being in love.

Perhaps slipping into such humdrum little intimacies, like a pet name, meant he was indeed in love. The idea made him smile, even if he had to allow it was an alien one. He hadn't known Theo long enough to know how he took his tea, much less long enough to spend years with him.

It did not matter, in the end. Since their attraction was deemed deviant, any love that existed because of it would take an unconventional form. Even as a child who realized he did not like girls, at least not *like that,* this had made sense to him and was not a deterrent.

Briefly, to parry the joy that followed the merest indication he might be nearer to love than he'd thought, he thought of the time he and David encountered one of David's Cambridge friends in The Alexandra. It was a pub in Norwich popular with young men, mostly working men, and he'd been wearing a coat that was at worst just old and somewhat dingy. He hadn't thought it would matter.

But David made some quip about his rag-picking acquaintance from Cromer, though Tom was not from Cromer, and the Cambridge friend with too much hair pomade chuckled as though they were both in the know about something Tom wouldn't understand.

After the friend had departed, David apologized and said sweet things about, in his words, rugged men.

Tom knew any kind of animal skin wouldn't fit his idea of how someone should look, especially a secretary. But Theo had never looked anything but immaculate, not even on the night they'd met when the cold might have necessitated some less fashionable choices.

"No," said Benson. "Well, I do think he took it. But I think he left it behind in the house. That would be easy, wouldn't it? It feels close. Very close. I don't think he took it with him, so yes, you're probably correct— he doesn't know what he has. He just didn't want Mr. Harper wearing it in society."

With a frown, Paul said, "He is a very unexciting creature, isn't he?"

"Very," said Tom quickly.

"How else can we all feel as though your Theo is still here?" asked Benson. "I haven't many encounters with a selkie to make proper inferences, but I'd bet my last few remaining teeth I'm right."

"He is not my Theo," said Tom. "And please don't bet your teeth when you have so few left at your disposal."

"I *said* a selkie was calling to you," said Benson, giving a little cackle. But he hadn't quite, not in as many words. "Anyway, he'd be yours if you asked." Peering at Tom's face, Benson added, "And *you* want to ask him. What is that, if not a silent call between you? My word, I do feel lucky I've always wanted women. Men are dense."

"That's not the only reason you should feel lucky," said Tom. Droll rather than defeatist, he added, "I'd consider the lack of risk for arrest quite lucky."

Paul spoke after a few moments of watching the fire, wisely sidestepping the conversation's present trajectory. "Your little theory could explain things, Benson. The selkie's not here, but the thing he needs most is."

About to object, Tom considered it. Such a small duplicity would be very easy to do without Theo knowing, not until they returned home and he noticed it was not present. "He might have taken it out of disdain. David has very exact ideas of how one should be outfitted, and I don't imagine they've become less particular in the years I haven't been speaking to him."

He did not want to explain that David did not like how he and Theo had got on, even though he had only encountered them together once. David could be in a mood to exercise some paltry little joke and very well might have executed this one without realizing anything more consequential about it.

Besides, he didn't want to believe David would be capable of intentionally depriving someone of his liberty. He might not like him, but that did not extend to supposing the worst possible motivations were present.

"What do you propose we do?" Paul asked Benson.

He tilted his head and chuckled once. "I expect the selkie may do something about it before we can. If we feel odd, imagine how he feels."

Like a delayed reaction to an acute physical injury, Tom started to have an influx of questions.

Paul had been keeping so much from him and he'd called Benson a sorcerer. Witch-hunter, he'd heard, but sorcerer was new. As was the insinuation that Paul *felt* things, which meant he might not be the only one in his family who could and did. He did not wish to think it had been purposefully kept from him, but it must have if Benson and Paul spoke of it so candidly now.

The only thing that had changed, though, was Theo. He was the new component for all of them, and even if he'd visited before, this had been the first time he'd met Tom and been to The Shuck.

Could Paul always sense him on the earlier visits? Why couldn't I? He swallowed a small twinge of envy. Well, he hadn't been here the last two or three winters, being occupied by other work, and Theo did not venture here during the summer because David did not.

His uncle read the perplexed look on his face and interpreted it without hesitation as Benson cackled again. "Come." He beckoned gently with his right hand. "You'll need a drink for all this."

The fascinating thing was, he rather thought he didn't. In some ways, all of this was more his element. It was the world as it was that posed the trouble. "I'll have some tea, if I'm to have anything at all."

If Paul was startled, he guarded it well, and Tom followed him up the stairs to the rooms that were dressed in dust.

18

They weren't actually as filthy as his childhood imagination led him to believe. There was dust, there was clutter, and there was an inordinate amount of papers almost as though Paul were a clandestine novelist, but the dust had not accrued in formidable piles. In the end, he supposed that was not how dust behaved anyway. Most of it was in the carpets, rising in small puffs when he took a step somewhere Paul did not.

"The chair there by the fireplace is clean," said Paul, turning on the old gas sconces set into the walls. It would have been the easiest thing in the room to keep somewhat clean, having neither upholstery nor cushions and being hewn of some kind of dense wood.

"Where did you get it? It looks like something an austere vicar would have to sit in," said Tom. Evidently, he was not to sit comfortably while they talked.

Paul chuckled, and for a moment, it took years from his countenance. "On the side of a quiet road near Thetford. I presume someone just left it."

Tom took his hand off the back of the chair. "You're sure it isn't haunted?"

"Surely you don't believe all the stories about the woods," said Paul, but he still looked young and puckish.

"So I'm not to believe those, but I'm to believe yours?" he replied with a smirk. "That's very selective." The Thetford chair felt neither foreboding nor dark, so he sat. "Go on, then. Tell me all of it."

"I don't know where to begin."

And this, thought Tom, was the thing that must have hindered Paul from being transparent at least as much as fear. His irritation waned, because he could understand that sense of absolute overwhelm, and he shrugged. "Anywhere."

In a practiced motion, Paul took a seat on a settee half-crowded by sheafs of paper without overturning any of them. What he chose to tell first was the story of a little boy who dreamt the family dog died, only to be reassured it was just a dream, an awful one.

The dog did die in the exact way he'd seen. Still, his mother said, a dream was only a dream.

The boy had another dream: his father hired a maid with ginger hair and lovely green eyes.

Within the next week, the same girl appeared in the taproom looking for a position.

And so on it went. After a few too many coincidences, the boy decided not to mention his dreams unless something terrible was going to happen to his family that he might prevent, because he tried talking about the dull ones until his mother and father had fewer reassurances that it was all just happenstance. As time passed, they exchanged more nervous glances.

"Your grandfather remarked, eventually, that I'd best not talk about them at school. The other children would think it was an odd thing, he told me, and he was probably right," Paul said. "I never tested it for myself. Granted, I did only try talking—about anything at all, not dreams—to one other boy whom I counted as a friend. Forget being shy, I was outright fearful. Scared of my own shadow."

"But they weren't *afraid* of you, Granny and Grandfather. Were they?"

"No, not really," said Paul. "They were never unkind about it. But from their perspectives, either I had some absurd talent or I was mad, so why would they encourage me to talk about what I could do?"

Tom inclined his head. "I would be afraid of how other people reacted to my child, but I wouldn't be frightened of a child who saw the future." He stopped and thought it over. "You don't see everything that's going to happen, do you?"

Even just thinking it made him quell a shudder. He had enough distress with ambient smells and emotions and the occasional colors, but at least that wasn't like seeing Benson tumble down a flight of stairs and snap his neck at the bottom.

"No, it's like. . . spiderwebs. I don't know if I'm the spider, but perhaps I am, and something tugs at a tendril until I see it. It's sporadic and I've never honed it, so it's never grown or become more precise. Nowhere near useful or terrifying enough that I could make a living off cards or bets, or save people from housefires or murders."

Or see Alistair dying. Tom did not have to say it because the thought lingered between them, heavy even if unspoken.

"Sometimes it can be good. Good things happen just as bad things do," said Paul quietly. He took a pause, then asked, "What is it like for you?"

"I don't see things that come to pass in my dreams."

"I didn't think so, which is why I spoke broadly."

His voice shaking a little, Tom said, "If you knew, if you thought there was any similarity, why did you never take me aside and explain it to me? I thought I was mad for years. Hell, Paul, I still do."

If he truly gave any consideration to what it might have been like to have someone understand his internal world at least a little, he would become too angry to speak prudently, so he tried to avoid wondering how his life might have been different had Paul extended some kind of guidance. He had not been so angry when he'd heard about the truth of Alistair's death, but he was angry about this.

"I thought it was all a curse after Alistair died," said Paul. He'd lowered his head and held his chin in his hand, still meeting Tom's eyes as his posture slumped with shame. "I didn't want to talk about Alistair and me, or you. Whatever you can do paired with who you are prone to love... the prospect of you going through life did scare me. It wasn't right, but I felt I could somehow influence you poorly if I took more involvement in raising you."

"But your life wasn't all bad! It isn't."

"It wasn't, and that's why it scared me. You could experience such wonderful things and have them ripped away overnight."

Trying to be gentle about it, Tom said, "But that could happen to anybody. Any person with no powers and nothing to mark them. It would have made a world of difference if you'd just spoken to me."

"Will you speak to me now, even if it's years too late?"

He appreciated being asked even though he would

say nothing but *yes*. If he was going to help Theo in any way, all he could bring to mind was locating his skin so that it could be returned to its owner, and he wanted to know more about all of this strange business. "Of course." He shook his head and glanced around. "If you will let me help you tidy this place up. I don't think a man who loved you would want you to live around his absence like this."

He hadn't really known Alistair as anyone but the man who was happy to introduce him to his first pint and teased his Uncle Paul when Paul grew surly over the day's books, but he did not think he'd wish for Paul to suffer even in the name of remembrance.

"Fine," said Paul, though he sounded faintly distressed at the prospect.

"Good," said Tom. He committed himself to the thing properly and tried to be succinct. He was still getting used to speaking to his uncle about so much. "I smell things that aren't there, and sometimes see colors that aren't there, and feel things that aren't mine. In fact, none of them are mine. They all belong to other people, and everyone has a... signature."

Not once in this entire strange evening of revelations had Tom seen Paul genuinely taken aback until now. His eyes wide, he said, "I only ever notice those on occasion. Certainly knew Alistair's. But that's why the perpetual. . ." he sat up straight, then made a drinking gesture with his right hand as though he was acting in a play.

Tom couldn't help but chuckle. "I always knew you were clever, but that's almost *too* perceptive of you. Drink does dampen it a bit."

"And is it easier for you to be on a boat or a dock somewhere?"

"Well, there are fewer people, so you'd think... but

often they're quite powerful personalities, my peers there. So... no, in other ways."

"Christ, now I really do regret never looking after you when you were a lad. You can learn to manage it better, you know."

He knew Paul didn't mean the drinking. "You sort of did."

Paul scoffed. "In the most minimal way I could. By putting you to work here."

"You were frightened, or grieving, or frightened and grieving." Happy to have broken through all these familial obscurities at last, but unsure how to navigate anything too emotional for Paul and having no desire to kindle his own bitterness should he delve too far, Tom asked, "How does Benson come into all of this?"

At that, his uncle stood and poured them each a finger of some brown spirit from an unassuming, simple crystal decanter. "Were you planning on retiring early tonight, or do you have some time?" The glassware was all serviceable and not dusty at all, but it didn't match what they kept downstairs. Tom looked at him quizzically. "This is all I drink, these days. It's from Alistair's favorite distillery. I always make sure to have a bottle on hand."

Tom accepted the whisky with enthusiasm. He needed a little fire in his blood, because he was pondering how to locate a selkie's skin and the evening was gloomy and cold.

First, he'd talk to Benson. Were there ways to find it without tearing a place asunder from wall to wall? It might be better to give it a night so he could think a little.

∼

RATHER THAN REMOVE the Mother Julian medal more often than he had to, because eventually he found Tom was right and the clasp's wee hinge was a little fussy, Theo kept it hidden under his collar or his nightshirt. It helped that even though he and David still shared a bed, they presently weren't engaging in anything more than exactly that.

He knew he should have given it back to Tom regardless of what the lad said, but on evenings after days like this when one of David's buyers or suppliers seemed to be on the prowl for a problem and wasn't likely to relent, he found it calming to surreptitiously fiddle with the chain. Anyway, he hadn't felt quite well since they'd come home, so it was helpful to have something meditative to do with his fingers even if he could only really do it when no one was looking in his direction.

He was alone for the moment, sitting at his desk in the office David had let on Upper St. Giles. It was clean and beautifully appointed, inspiring confidence in all who visited. Unfortunately, because he knew David would likely return in a state of indignation, it held little comfort for him. He worried little for himself. In fact, he didn't worry at all for himself.

But the thought of working through some kind of trivial business matter while David was in a foul mood was almost unbearable.

More precisely, it really was the idea of helping *David* process the trivial business matter that felt unbearable. Unbidden, he thought of helping Tom solve something silly and mundane at The Shuck, and how he felt about the prospect changed. He would no doubt enjoy the task in that case.

The front door, separated from the office by a small vestibule, gave an audible and deathly creak that only happened if one pushed it too far back. It closed and Theo waited. Then the office door swung open to admit David, who swept off his hat and placed it carefully on an unoccupied brass hook.

"Well?" said Theo, figuring he might as well get it over with and dive right into the matter at hand, so to speak.

"Nothing."

"Your expression and the creaking door don't seem like nothing."

"I don't know how Father managed to keep these people happy." David scrubbed at his face and Theo had to resist telling him he should at least wash his hands before he did.

"I don't think he did," said Theo, offering up a smirk. "He wasn't exactly a man of the people."

"No, you are right about that," said David from behind his hands. "Still, he must have done something right. I feel as though they're often waiting for me to budge on every little matter because I am not him."

Reserving his words on what he thought about that, Theo remained silent as he decided what to say. If he insisted that David was unlike his father, which he really was—and being unlike him was a good thing, in his estimation—it might be taken as a challenge, the wrong kind of dissention.

Even though David *also* didn't seem to want to be like his father at all.

It was a very confusing matter and having known him long enough to say, Theo wanted to advise David to go into some environment that was much more intellectual. He enjoyed history, and talking to all the old folks he encountered even if they were absolute strangers, and he could talk for days about all those pilfered ancient artifacts at the British Museum. Why shouldn't he be a man of research if that was what he liked?

He could hire another person to manage his father's business and benefit from the profits without having to engage in something he didn't much enjoy. Plenty of men who didn't have to make their own living did things of the kind.

"Have you ever thought of letting someone else manage all this?"

David's long fingers fell from his mouth and he said, "How do you mean?"

"Precisely what I say." Theo nodded to the ledgers before him. "You have more than enough money coming in that it would not be out of the question to hire some kind of manager to, well, manage things." He knew David was not generally advised to do anything differently than he did it, because he struck most people as a stern fellow who was set in his ways. The sternness was a façade that hid outright anxiety, for when he allowed himself to be less stern, he was far more genial but far more prone to needing reassurance.

The sky was darkening outside and he listened to a few passersby on the street as David seemed to mull over his suggestion. "I had never thought of it." Thankfully, he presently allowed himself to be less stern.

Theo chuckled quietly, then cleared his throat of the hoarseness that had lingered since they arrived back from Cromer just about a fortnight ago. "No, I know. But, truly, David, I think you might be more content if you just stepped aside a little. Have a care for your own happiness." He didn't think David had ever really cared much for it.

"But what would I do?"

"Well, do not sound so lost, for you would still have the final say here. On all things cloth-related, you would be king. The only difference would be someone else seeing to all the daily logistics."

"I understand that, but what would I do with my time?"

"Would that we could all be so lucky to ask that," said Theo cheerfully. "Anything, of course. I was thinking you could do some research and come up with a monograph."

"A monograph?"

"Yes, a book devoted to a narrow subject. It goes into useless detail that no one else cares about, except for the devotees of said narrow subject." With a smile, Theo closed the ledgers and began to tidy his desk, straightening inkstands and paper. "Think on it. I have known you long enough to see it isn't that you're badly suited to this. Obviously you've been well-trained to do it. But it does nothing for your soul and mostly just puts you in a bad mood, to be frank."

"I know what a monograph is, you rogue." When Theo glanced at him, he was smiling. "I suppose I would have enough money to hire a manager, now that you have mentioned the idea. Someone who perhaps has a storefront, knows the cloth trade from that end."

"That does rule me out. I can balance your books, but do not expect me to liaise with all these weavers and the like you keep telling me about." Rather salt of the earth lot, from the sound of it, and some of them did not come from Norwich directly and never let David forget they had travelled to see him or spent more money to correspond with him.

While the city had once boasted a local cloth industry that notably produced inexpensive and popular paisley to compete with the real thing, much of the manufacture had dwindled by now. That was where the Mills before David made their money. Who would have thought descendants of disreputable witch-hunters had also made paisley to subvert that of Paisley itself.

In the later years of the previous century, Norwich had taken up chocolate, of all things, as well as Colman's mustard. And he couldn't forget about all the shoemakers. They'd been part of local industry for years and years.

Well, leaving aside all thoughts of such disparate foods as chocolate and mustard, or such odd mates as witch-hunters and those who made cloth, the weavers might exasperate even him and he considered himself something of a diplomat. A pencil rolled off the desk and clattered to the floor, giving him a second to pause as he captured it and replaced it in a drawer.

When he straightened, it allowed him to realize that David peered at him with an abnormal expression, one close to regret. His charming features were creased with remorse, or what looked like it.

"What is it?"

"Nothing. You just never cease to have the most wonderful ideas." Some imperative sentiment seemed to die before it could use David's tongue to speak, and he sighed. "I wondered if. . ."

"Yes?"

"I wanted to. . ." David frowned. "That is, I think we need. . . *I* need to say. . ."

The seeming guilt paired with this evident apprehension made Theo nervous. But he had to remind himself that he also had important topics to broach with David and had not managed to do so, largely because he dreaded the potential for conflict and any

truths that might result from it. He abhorred starting
and trailing off with no productive end in sight, too,
and could abide it in others but always felt it made
him seem foolish if he did not know exactly what
to say.

The office's normally serene atmosphere was
starting to grate and he made his tone intentionally
soft to combat the churning he felt inside. "What did
you want? You can tell me."

David cleared his throat. "Nothing at all. Never
mind."

Yet it sounded very much like something and Theo
could not divine what was being unsaid. While he
knew it was unfair to hold David to any standards he
could not meet himself, he couldn't help but wish he'd
start these difficult conversations first.

But perhaps he was just feeling under the weather.

～

HE REALIZED his instincts were slipping, and he was
worse off than he thought, when it took him almost
the full fortnight after leaving Cromer and arriving in
Norwich to realize his skin hadn't come with him. It
had taken over a week to admit he felt unwell, and by
the time he'd done so, he still hadn't made the connection between his skin and his illness. By the second
week, though, he began to wonder.

To be fair, these kinds of separation felt at first like
a flu or terrible cold, so he assumed he might be
dealing with one of those. A longer life did not mean
one was immune to colds, flus, or anything at all. It
just meant, should one be so lucky—or unlucky, depending on who was judging—there was the potential
of outliving peers, friends, lovers, enemies. Anyone

who happened to be ordinary, which was largely everyone with only a few exceptions.

What happened after the flu or cold stage depended on the reason for being separated from the skin. If it was a willing or innocent reason, the ill-feelings mellowed and abated entirely when the skin was brought back into proximity with its owner. There were some situations that fit that bill and they could happen: forgetting the skin at home while one made a few days' journey, or letting someone sleep under it for a day or two, those sorts of things. The latter might be highly specific to a good friend, a lover, or a family member.

If the reason was disingenuous, he'd been told, the feeling of being ill mutated into an unrelenting itch, a restless disconnect between mind and body.

Like the one he presently experienced.

Additionally, since he had left it in the bottom of his oldest and handiest portmanteau, he'd assumed it would be safe because nobody would know to look for it, or go through his things for some other reason, and either lose it or take it. In general, he was happy to take care of his own belongings and any of the maids or butlers knew it.

He'd been wrong about one or both of those assumptions, but kept consoling himself with the thought that nobody knew what the skin was. He simply had not told anyone, and that solved that. It was lonely never to divulge part of one's identity, but he believed the risks outweighed the potential gains.

I was never tempted to until I met Tom.

Which, in turn, actually meant he had been wrong about several things: what David truly meant to him, what he liked, what he wanted. Hindsight was damnable.

"Fuck," he said to the empty room and all the world.

If he did not have it, he could not be with Tom at all. *Losing* it would be one thing, for he supposed he could muddle along in whatever relationship he chose and all would simply be lackluster until he expired. If that was not the definition of most average lives, he did not know what else was. But his entire body told him this was not an act of forgetfulness or misplacing something.

Theo had been very fortunate. No one had ever spitefully taken his skin, so he was in the wilds of guesswork. Father had once encouraged him to leave it behind while they made a trip to Edinburgh to visit a family friend and he'd done so to understand what it would feel like to be separated. In the end, it had not felt good by anyone's measure and he'd taken two days in bed recovering from the several days that were meant to be for leisure. He was glad he'd done it for experience's sake, but the memory was not a fond one.

David. It had to be.

Just last night, had there not been something on the tip of his tongue? He was the only person Theo lived with, the sole individual who had seen almost all —if not all—of his possessions, and he'd passed re-marks about *that awful thing*. Without knowing the *awful thing* was responsible for a fair amount of Theo's overall health and autonomy.

Somehow, and Theo did not quite know how, David had done something with the skin. *But not inno-cently.* Was it possible to do something unkindly, but without knowing how impactful the spiteful action was? He couldn't make up his mind about what might be better. . . David willfully trapping him, or David not knowing he could be trapped and managing to do it anyway because he was being petty and just didn't like the look of a certain possession.

Was he going to admit to it, but lost his nerve in the moment?

If so, Theo could sympathize.

"If this was to be the end result, I should have told the truth all along."

Nothing but a shout from outside answered him, and it was not even directed toward him at all. Life went on around him for others, he supposed, even if his own felt momentarily suspended.

Wherever the skin was, it must be intact or he would not be here staring at the cheerful, green Chapelfield Gardens on a bright day. On one occasion, Father had remarked they could die like anyone else, but the most thorough way to do it was by destroying their skins. Having been just sixteen at the time he heard it, Theo was suitably impressed and irrevocably disturbed by the notion.

Well, perhaps not irrevocably. He did not dwell on the thought now, but he'd obsessed about it for years before finally concluding that if he were to die in such a manner, maybe it was meant to happen just as a carriage accident or some kind of illness could also end his life. His ordinary was simply different from other people's, that was all.

Through the sitting room's window that overlooked the gardens, he watched a small child toddle from her adept governess as he considered his options. He did not believe David actually understood what he'd done. No, David was not quite fanciful enough for it. All he knew was a gray fur happened to be important to Theo, but because it did not meet his aesthetic standards and Theo had recently peeved him a bit, it had been silently, unceremoniously left aside.

They'd played such little games before, but never with any high stakes.

David had taken the last digestive in the tin; Theo hid his favorite pen. Theo had accidentally poked David in the eye while asleep and stretching; David "borrowed" his favorite cufflinks the next time they went out to dine. They'd usually laughed about such things.

Theo could not chart when they'd stopped laughing and started feeling fraught and tired.

So this little game was not exactly out of the ordinary, but it had unfortunate ramifications.

What *had* changed was his new acquaintance with Tom. It was a new familiarity David did not like and yet seemed deeply fascinated by, although it was possible Theo was mistaking envy for fascination. Maybe it was both. When one had been so maltreated as David, it seemed they could not adroitly display or manage their inner world and so it manifested in a tangled fashion. Any charged emotion with considerable weight, like dread or bitterness, was often legible to others as a brand of avid intensity rather than what it was.

He thought suddenly of Cromer and of the only time he'd seen Tom and David in the same place, which was in the taproom in The Shuck. It was obvious how much had been left unsaid between them when they parted ways because of what David's father had witnessed in his house.

The house. Had Theo been an excitable sort of man, he'd have snapped his fingers at the thought entering his head.

If the skin was not in his portmanteau, which it

was not, it had to be in the Mills' second home by the sea. David was so fixed in his travel habits he was like the Tube or an old train route, so it was implausible he'd deviate in any significant manner simply to rid himself of a sartorially offensive personal possession. Besides, they had not been parted for any substantial length of time since well before Christmas. What Theo was missing would not be anywhere but somewhere David already tread.

If it was, he would be quite surprised. With a wee flare of hope flickering in his heart, he put his mind to an immediate trip back to Cromer.

19

The night after he'd ventured up to Paul's flat, Tom decided to take a little thieving jaunt to the empty Mills residence. He thought about sitting down with his uncle again and simply talking to him, and trusting Theo to do whatever he needed to do.

But it did not suit him to take no action, even if taking this exact action still felt a little mad.

While he wished to spend more time with Paul and no doubt would in light of how much the tenor of their interactions had changed, he had a goal in mind and would not delay it. Besides, Paul was obviously knackered from relaying so much information at one time. They could not undo years of reserve in one or two evenings without succumbing to exhaustion, and besides, Tom needed time to decide how he felt about everything.

It was not every day one learned one's desired paramour was a creature of tales, or one's uncle was a clandestine seer, or that one's uncle's friend was a witch-hunter given to knowing almost everything that went on around him. Before setting out, he'd cornered

Benson downstairs. He was in the far corner of the taproom smoking a noxious tobacco that might have been something else besides tobacco, and he seemed to expect Tom.

"Pull up a pew, lad."

Tom did not take the actual suspected pew that roved around the taproom depending on who wished to sit in it, but instead sat the wrong way round on a chair and crossed his arms over the back of it, eyeing Benson. "I want to take that skin and give it back to Theo. How do I find it?" He added, "Are you certain it's in the house?"

"Well, we're within the realms of conjecture because I have never dealt with a situation like this one, but to the best of my measure, I'd guess it is. Either that or it could be anywhere in town."

Tom blanched. "I don't even want to imagine it is." Then he thought of David's habits when they'd been better acquainted and could not picture him going to all the trouble of actively discarding something anywhere but a location that was convenient.

"It is about, somewhere, otherwise he'd be dead."

"Theo?" His alarm rose again. "Would be *dead?*"

"Your selkie, yes."

"Stop saying it," Tom said. But he was not really so peeved. Just still reeling, somewhat.

"Very well, I'll refrain." Benson exhaled a long breath of white smoke and Tom tried not to breathe too much of it in, waving a hand to disperse it slightly. "Some lore says destroying it would kill them, just like keeping the skin would trap them. Besides, don't you think you'd know if he died?"

"I shan't think of it." In point of fact, Tom believed he would, but Benson could not be shown to be right about all of his suppositions. He rubbed a little at his own hair, which he knew was hopelessly mussed because he could not stop unthinkingly playing with it. "Do I do anything special to locate it once I'm inside?"

"Like a magical Morris dance?"

"If that's what it takes, it's not as though anyone would see me," said Tom, rather put out that Benson was making quips. "But I'm not one for dancing of any sort, so whether it's a waltz or a reel I'm supposed to do, I'd likely fail."

Yielding, likely interpreting Tom's caustic tone as belying his nerves, Benson used his tongue and lips to resettle his pipe to one corner of his mouth. "No. I expect you'd be able to find it faster than anyone but Mr. Harper. Don't blunt how you see and feel. Have you been drinking tonight?"

Taking in Benson's words and impatient to set out, he said swiftly, "No, not much."

"Good." Having little more to add, it seemed, Benson said, "Good luck. I think it will go well for you."

Tom did not know about that. But as he approached the house and all was peaceful and Theo felt very near, he wondered if luck might be on his side after all. David's wasn't far from The Shuck and it occupied enough land that its most immediate neighbors were a small bluff and the sea. Other houses' lights shone like little ships on the water, but none were so close that he was concerned about being caught. So long as he did not tarry near any windows with a candle, which he wasn't even sure he'd be able to find, he'd be fine. Luckily, he could see very well in the dark and the night was clear, so he counted on not needing one.

He had not made a career out of being a petty

thief, so he did not know the best way to go about breaking into anybody's house. A lack of human neighbors would make it much easier and the rushing waves masked many small sounds. Stopping at one of the side gates to collect himself, he looked at the dark windows, discounting any above the ground floor, and evaluated the plain door nearest him.

Yes, it might be the best way of entry.

~

LIKE A MAN FLEEING a murderer who chased him with a blunt hatchet, Theo all but sprinted to The Shuck when he got close, desperate enough not to make it seem like a visit for a customary reason.

Even as the train had come closer, he had started to feel marginally better, then once he arrived in the town proper, almost back to the full of health. Something still nagged at him as out of place, but he could ignore it much more easily. If he hadn't suspected what he did, he'd just attribute the feeling to a bad night of little sleep or needing to eat a meal.

When he entered The Shuck to see a man very like Tom—svelte but wiry under his clothes, hazel eyes tinged with more olive, deeper lines around them, same umber hair—he didn't even bother trying to employ niceties with him. It had to be Tom's uncle, which meant there were certain things he would infer and certain tells Theo most likely could not hide from him.

It simply wasn't done to burst into an establishment demanding to know where someone was, for example, probably not with any level of fervor but certainly not with his own as it was in the moment. He wanted Tom to help him and admitted it was an act of desperation. Any number of things could go wrong and he had not even explained himself or what he needed. He was just compelled to seek him because he did not wish to be alone, and he wanted him, and he was tired of trying to be decent.

He rounded on Tom's uncle, anyway. "Is he here?"

Straight dark eyebrows drew together as the somberly-dressed man paused mid-step near the entryway's desk. He was named Paul, if Theo remembered properly. "I assume you mean my nephew?"

Theo nodded. "Mr. Theodore Harper. I beg your pardon, Mr. Apollyon, but is he working?"

"I know who you are." Well, that was either encouraging or ominous, but Theo noticed he did have a slight dimple that might have indicated a hidden smile before he made his declaration. Encouraging, then. "He's stepped out."

Crestfallen, Theo said, "May I ask when he might return?"

Of all the nights, Tom had to be out on this particular one. He supposed he could comb the beaches for a lone despondent man built like a Classical athlete, or hang around outside the old cottage where he'd confirmed the lone despondent man was indeed built like a Classical athlete because he'd seen him half-undressed. If Tom was not here, Theo expected he might be in either of those places.

He had first set eyes upon him at a wee bookshop run by a woman called Mrs. Florence Mattingly, but that was closed this time of night. He brushed aside the memory of meeting his gaze there in the shop, and fixed his attention upon Mr. Apollyon.

"He didn't say." Mr. Apollyon evaluated him with some sharpness. "Is it urgent?"

"Unfortunately, yes, and I do think he can help

me." That finessed the truth a little, but it didn't matter.

The dubious chimney man who'd claimed Theo might abscond with the silver if Tom did not watch him appeared, bringing with him a reeking pipe and a half-full glass of some golden ale. Theo glanced at the pipe. He loved to smoke his, but did not want to guess what was in this one.

"Can he, now? What with?" This evening, he wore a hat shaped like a bucket that might have once been brown waxed cotton, but it was now so battered and maltreated it looked swampy black under the gaslight.

"Benson," said Mr. Apollyon. It was hard to tell if it was a chide, a warning, or a chuckle. His face was too hard to read and his tone had not changed much.

"I regret to say it is a personal matter," said Theo, praying for patience. He'd done it, now, for assuredly both of them would take that as a double entendre. It had just slipped out of him. *Would that it was so simple as wanting to confirm a meeting point for* that.

"Oh, we're well-versed in those," said Benson. He drank some of his ale, sticking his pipe carefully in a wide shirt pocket. It might singe its way out if he was not careful.

For a transitory and outrageous moment, Theo tried to picture him and Mr. Apollyon together. It wouldn't necessarily have been the strangest thing he'd seen, but it would have been odd indeed. He glanced from Benson to Mr. Apollyon, questioning without vocalizing.

Mr. Apollyon gave the tiniest shake of his head and allowed a slip of an actual smile to appear.

"I'd wager not this one," Theo said.

"And do you wager often, then, selkie? I'd refrain

from taking it up if you think you're any good, because you're wrong."

At that, Mr. Apollyon brought his hands to his mouth in a gesture of weary incredulity, his eyebrows going up instead of drawing together again. "You old coot, you're subtle as a battering ram," he said, still hiding his mouth so the words were muffled.

Apparently unbothered by the reproach, Benson shrugged and watched Theo for a reaction. Theo got the sense Benson liked to jolt people.

Unfortunately for Benson, he wasn't easy to shock and had been surprised enough times that he now had to allocate where to spend it. If he'd learned anything, it was that people were actually not all that predictable even if they could be interpreted to a certain extent.

Circumstances could be understood like tides, but people's choices were not so easy to fathom even if you could surmise some of them before they happened. This business with his skin was a good example of that, for although he could see how David had probably landed him in the trouble he was in, nothing was quite as it seemed.

He'd grown up being cautioned against letting people into his innermost truths for fear this very thing would occur, it had occurred anyway, and where did that leave him? Similarly, his father had been crushed by his mother's actions without her knowing arguably the most crucial thing about him.

"I knew there was *something* about you as soon as I saw you," Theo said, much more tired than he was angry, thinking back to late December when he'd first encountered Benson behind the reception desk in the entryway.

Now he assessed all the bits about Benson's demeanor that marked him as off-kilter and esoteric, eyes remaining on the small twinkles of brass and silver among his scarf and lapels, some hidden near the ends of his gray shoulder-length hair as though they were woven into it. All, if one truly looked at them, were tiny runes and symbols, the likes of which he didn't know.

He did not understand what or whom he was looking at, exactly, but he could make a decent guess that it was someone who liked wee charms and sigils. It was also someone who did not spend much time in society, or at least the kind of society on which the world turned.

He could not help but like him.

Really, Theo had one question alone. He could think about origins and intents later.

"Does he know?" Though he should have addressed Benson, who'd raised the issue, he looked more at Mr. Apollyon, whose mouth opened but did not give the first reply. "Does Silence—Tom—know about me?"

"He does because I told him," Benson said.

Theo sighed, glancing at the ceiling above his head. "Of course you did." He thought of his gentle Mr. Drunkard and had to have faith it hadn't put him off, or put ideas into his head. That was, if he'd believed Benson in the first place. Some people might. He probably had.

Then Theo remembered the great assurance with which Tom had said stealing a selkie's skin would be unconscionable, and it helped him avoid panic. While he hadn't brought up the subject because he'd wanted Tom to know—or thought he might make an inference—perhaps some small part of him had hoped he would. The much larger part knew most people, even people who'd spent their lives near the sea or reading novels, wouldn't make that leap.

But Tom was not most people. It was trite to say he saw it in his eyes, but he saw it there, a little, as well as in how he spoke, breathed, and carried himself.

"The knowledge is safe with him," said Mr. Apollyon.

Swallowing, Theo brought his head back to a normal position and looked at him. "Is it?"

"Yes," he said. "*You're* safe with him."

How he ached to believe that. Tom's uncle manifestly did. "So. He didn't think you were mad, or joking." If he wasn't so intent upon letting himself into David's house and figuring out if his skin was there after all, he'd probably wait for Benson and Mr. Apollyon to reveal more about what kind of people they were. But his mood did not permit the practicality or the curiosity.

He had heard witches and seers often made a study of their fellows, while some others chose to make a profession of preternatural creatures. Father had been more accustomed to these underground circles than he was, so despite knowing this, it was all theoretical. He'd never met a declared witch on his own, just been introduced to a few friends of Father's who happened to be magical. On the face of it, they were what one might expect out of anybody who lived in a city. They had trades, jobs, and lives that did not necessarily mark them as any different than their neighbors.

"He did not. Not at all."

No, that did not strike him as unusual for Tom. "Do you truly not know where he is?"

Because his mind was half a hop from utter anxiety, it was also close to petulantly insisting Tom must be with whoever he'd been with in the cottage, even though the same thought had just come to him without eliciting such an infantile reaction.

On closer reflection, he would mind very much if it were the case and part of him was glad he was capable of such envy, because David roused practically none. He tried to picture David in the arms of another and succeeded, but it didn't make him feel the same stab of heartache. Instead, it made him feel peculiarly free, as though David should be with someone who was not him.

"I am sorry," said Mr. Apollyon, "but I don't. I did not ask. All he told me was he would be out for some time, possibly quite late."

After leaving enough time for Theo to feel nebulously lost, then just internally admit he needed to do the thing himself and this was all romantic folly, Benson said, "I do."

Both Theo and Mr. Apollyon looked at him with considerable shades of resignation. "Please tell the poor man where to find him, then," said Mr. Apollyon. "I should make sure Maeve hasn't set fire to my taproom again. She's just back from London and I really must mind her."

Benson watched him go, then hefted himself up to sit on the top of the desk.

"Again?" Theo could not help but ask, though it was the least important thing they could consider. Not if The Shuck caught fire this very instant, he supposed. Then it would be pertinent and none of them would need to worry about much except for the nearest point of exit.

"Oh, yes, she's reckless with the candles after she's had a couple of rounds, is dear Maeve, and her customary seat is right near some curtains." Wiggling his feet, and Theo was not taken aback when he realized how mucky Benson's well-worn shoes were, he folded his hands in his lap. "Right. Tom is off to the old Mills house. We only just spoke about it."

That was not what he expected to hear and he gaped at Benson. "Why?"

The house was empty until David next chose to use it, which might well be no sooner than this coming winter. He knew the caretaker David hired would make certain the property would not be damaged or broken into, and he would also feed Mary the mouser because she was not terribly proficient at mousing. But all that had nothing to do with Tom.

Unless, of course, he attracted the caretaker's attention. The man lived in rooms over the carriage house, though, so he might be able to sneak in without being discovered depending on where he entered. With luck, he would choose the right place.

Fortuitously, Musgrave the overzealous footman who'd been scarred by his military involvement had elected to move to Norwich and continue working for Mr. Mills, which might result in an innocent citizen being accidentally shot if he had one of his turns. People were much closer together there.

"You."

"Me?"

"I see *that's* got your tongue, a bit," said Benson. "Surprised?"

"Indeed, very much so."

"I supposed your skin might be in the house and mentioned it to both the Apollyons."

Several questions competed to be asked and Theo had to choose one. He was not often so eager to ask them, preferring instead to wait and see how events and information unfolded before him. Some called it indolent, but he'd found it was often a wise choice to delay.

"How the hell did you know that?" He shook his head, moving on to his second question. "How do you know. . . anything?" Then to his third. "How does Mr. Apollyon know it? Senior, I mean to say."

"Oh, that."

"Yes, that."

"Don't you think you ought to hurry over and make sure the younger has managed his task?" Whatever was happening in the taproom, it did not involve unwanted fire because there were no shouts of alarm or telltale draughts of smoke, but it was shrill and boisterous. They both looked toward the doorway, the sound quieted somewhat, and Benson finished his pint in two large swallows. "Trade is picking up. Think he's broken his streak of bad luck."

"I shall go, but not before you answer me."

"I'm a witch-hunter. Was taught it from the cradle, more or less. Mr. Paul Apollyon is a witch, also more or less. We are friends," said Benson with admirable and maddening succinctness. There was some charming skillfulness to stating things like this so pithily. "I can sense you, if you will, because you are not strictly without magic of your own. But I know a lot of things, me."

"Then Tom is one, too?" It might change things a little to have some common ground in that manner, if that was not just wishful thinking on his part. He had never been with anyone who was not purely typical, so far as he knew, but he also knew he'd never found anyone he wanted to grow old with. *Or watch grow old, rather.* He'd watch Tom get older while he aged in longer increments. "He's a witch?"

Benson's answer to that was the lift of his shoulder

paired with two words, and Theo had to take him at that. "Might be."

"How... what... are his talents?"

A cackle answered the question first, but Benson said, "He'd not call them talents. Feeling, sensing, knowing."

"I have never known any myself," said Theo, reflecting, "witches, I mean."

"You might well have and not known it. Does everyone know precisely who you are, then?"

There was very little he could say in rebuttal to that, so he did not. "He's at the Mills' home, now, you said?"

"I would not worry that he means to keep your skin for himself." Silent, for it was not natural to him to trust anyone that way even though he devoutly wanted to trust Tom, Theo tilted his head as Benson delivered another pronouncement. "I shan't let anyone check on you until the morning."

"Check on us?"

Another one of those shrugs that Benson apparently so liked to deploy preceded his speech. "What if the caretaker finds you and detains you? I assume there is such a man on the property."

"He won't."

"Even if you intend to sleep the night with him?" Benson was like the cat who got the cream, more self-satisfied than Mary eating the cheese meant to attract mice to a trap. There was no ambiguity as to who *him* was. But worse, the thought had not crossed his mind until the irascible witch-hunter put it there. Now that it had traipsed in, he'd have a hell of a time forcing it back out.

He did mean to do the thing properly, and for him,

that meant trying to communicate with David first. Not that he was any good at initiating it, clearly.

Nettled, he merely grunted in reply and resorted to an abrupt exit, not that he thought Benson would mind. Without thanking him, he left The Shuck and turned down the lane, heading for the road that led to David's.

20

Tom had just crossed the threshold into a disused bedroom when he heard a stealthy noise downstairs. His heartbeat quickened, then lodged in his throat. Imagination might have been getting the better of logic, but it suggested someone trying to close the main doors quietly without being noticed. He froze and tried to believe he'd imagined the insignificant creaks and clicks, for it would be unexpected indeed if someone else had broken in on the very same night.

Also, he doubted a burglar would be as courteous as he had been. He'd picked a lock on the servants' door to the kitchen because it was not on the same side as the carriage house, where providence led him to notice a gentle light pass behind one of the curtains in the rooms above it. Someone was in residence, and it had been rash not to consider if there would be. It wasn't unheard of for these larger homes to have a person or two present at all times while their owners were elsewhere.

You are letting your mind get the best of you.

Even though he chided himself, he let his senses reach out, thankful he was lucid enough to direct them. If someone else was here, maybe he'd notice them. But all he registered was Theo, which only told him he was—perhaps—on the correct path to attaining his goal. There would be no reason that he'd be feeling him unless the skin was nearby, and the sensation had only strengthened since he'd left The Shuck.

He waited for a handful of moments with his back to the door as he observed the bed and large, curtained window. Though he concentrated on what he could hear, there was nothing beyond the faint break of waves outside and the house settling against the omnipresent wind.

Then, despite the absurdity of the idea, he wondered if the place was haunted. Someone didn't have to die in a house for it to hold a ghost, or so he'd been given to believe from all the stories, and chances were Mr. Mills hadn't expired here. But it would be just his luck for the man to cause him trouble from the afterlife.

How could he believe in witches, or selkies, or witch-hunters—or himself—and not a ghost? Debating internally, he turned to go out of the room and check if there was a fellow intruder or perhaps a specter, not knowing what he might do if the latter appeared. He was in a mood to laugh out of nerves or spite, which he didn't think would please a spirit.

But when he looked squarely at the doorway, he gasped and did not get far at all.

A shadow lingered against the flat backdrop of the gloomy corridor, and it was poised to step inside and join him.

∾

THAT STARTLED breath punctuated the house's quiet like a streak of lighting against an ominous sky. Where there'd been only the beach and waves for noise, there was Tom heaving a gasp as though he'd just been hit in the stomach.

"Hush, no, it's only me." Theo put both of his hands up to pacify him and studied him as well as he could in the feeble light. It was almost too dark to see anything beyond the stark outlines of furniture and drop cloths, but as he waited for his eyes to adjust, he could see more. He spoke quickly, but quietly. "I've come back. I've had a set of keys for ages. David never minded, so I just kept them."

His body insisted he fling himself at the man and demanded to know why he did not. Instead of giving in, he stood immobile, arbitrating between the needs to placate him, pleasure him, or ascertain why he had really come. Part of the problem was, if he acted on what he felt, he would not do those things in that precise order no matter how prudent it was.

"Christ," said Tom, still breathing fast.

Theo lowered his hands. "I'm sorry. I thought you would know it was me." After he said it, he remembered that Tom would have no knowledge of what his uncle had divulged, or what Theo and Benson had discussed. He now knew that Tom was capable of sensing things beyond the usual ways of most people, but Tom didn't know what he'd learned.

His assertion did not seem to make a difference or it didn't register. "Never mind that, how did you make it up those old stairs without so much as a bloody creak?"

"Practice," said Theo. He would not detail how much practice or to what end, but most of it was to avoid Mr. Mills' notice. Even if he was not entirely able to understand anything that went on around him, from what was going to be served at dinner to his beloved horse being given to a distant cousin because David could not handle the creature, and his father could no longer safely ride for either transport or leisure. It had seemed like good form not to parade about with their actual intentions.

Tom nodded, raking fingertips through his untidy hair in that endearing habit of his. He'd gone out with no hat, and that testified to the haste with which he'd left The Shuck. "That would make sense." He took a few steps closer to Theo and said, "I am happy to see you, although I don't know if *happy* is the correct word to use under these circumstances."

"I understand." Though, no, *happy* was an understatement. He still wanted to test the limits of trust and hear from Tom himself that the skin was not his to keep, that he would be giving it back. He had yet to hear anything of the kind, but was so warmed by his presence that he could momentarily put his qualms aside.

"You don't seem taken aback to find me."

Crossing the threshold just to be near to him, Theo said, "I'm not. I went to The Shuck first."

"Why?" Tom followed his every move, intent upon him, and the scrutiny felt wonderful.

"Oh, I rather think we both know the answer to that," Theo said. "You. You were the only one who would do for me. I wanted your help or at least your company while I helped myself." He thought it best not to sit on the bed, for who knew what they might get up to on a bed, so he sat upon a massive antique chest at the foot of it. "As to why I wanted that, well, I can speculate."

Tom smiled, gazing down at him. "I like being your object of speculation."

"And Mr. Benson told me you had come here." The smile dimmed and Theo hastened to reassure him. "He told me why. It's all right. Events have not been what I was expecting—at all—but it really is all right." What he didn't say was, it was only going to be all right if Tom was unlike so many of his compatriots, who would rather possess and subdue something than foster a reciprocal and potentially lovely relationship.

"I didn't know before he told me." Tom's words were spoken quietly, hesitance writ large in them. "On my word, I didn't. All I knew was, you felt new and. . . wonderful, but I wasn't angling to come here for any nefarious reasons. I don't want to capture you." He took a pause, then said, "Benson might have known what you were the entire time, from the first time he spoke to you. That jibe about the silver and all." With an expression of fierce protectiveness, he finished, "But I shouldn't think he'd harm you, either."

Presently, Theo was not thinking about whether Benson might or might not harm him. He knew he would not, though was also moved Tom believed he needed the comfort. "Why did you break into this house, then? Why rush here under cover of night when I'm sure you could surmise I would have to come back myself?"

Giving a hangdog half-smile, Tom said, "I did not quite think it through, but I knew you were in trouble and that was enough to push me. I doubted David would have known what. . . who. . . you were."

"*Who* is fine, though it may also be *what*," said Theo. "I'm not bothered. I don't even know, myself. Doubt anyone does, if I'm being honest."

Tom nodded once and continued. "I just didn't think you'd have confided in him, having seen how you acted around each other. Never mind how you spoke about him." It was true that he'd never spoken about David like a man besotted, Theo thought, amused. He pursed his lips and kept the sentiment to himself while Tom still spoke. "But I did believe Benson when he told us he thought the... fuck, this is an extraordinary conversation... ah, what you needed was in the house all along."

Grumbling, but with some respect due to the old man, Theo said, "He's an astute one."

"Is it here, then? I don't know if I should trust myself." Trepidation colored Tom's voice.

"Even though you went to all the trouble of, I assume, picking a lock?"

"Better that than breaking a window or kicking something in, just in case. I saw a light above the carriage house, so I came in through the kitchen."

"There's a caretaker, but so long as we don't make too much noise, I expect he's probably having a nice evening in and won't have cause to suspect we're even in the house." Fondly, wishing to cut through the doubt that suffused Tom's demeanor even as he waited for his own doubts to be addressed, he said, "I used to sneak in that way, too. Did you see Mary on your way up?"

"Mary?"

"You would notice her. Very pretty girl. Then again, maybe *you* wouldn't." Careful not to tease too much, Theo smiled instead of carrying on. It wasn't kind to prod at him, even if he was quite endearing when flustered.

Already flummoxed, Tom was growing more confused as Theo spoke. He chewed at his lip, then said,

"No one else is here. I *did* think you might be Mr. Mills' ghost come to haunt me for a moment, but nobody else is in the house. I saw no one."

"Mary is a cat, not no one."

With a spluttering chuckle, Tom said, "You didn't think to take her to Norwich?"

"No, because Ernest isn't ready for a lady friend. Or any kind of friend."

"I assume Ernest is a cat and not a man."

Sitting back on the chest until his spine met the footboard behind him, Theo nodded. Now that he'd arrived at the house and knew without a doubt his skin was somewhere within it, the physical effects of that proximity were taking hold and felt far less ill than he had in days. He could think more clearly, too. "He is a very sweet creature unless you are any sort of dog, another cat, or a feather duster. David wanted to take Mary with us, but in the end he decided against it because she's from here and Ernest would never stand for a companion. The caretaker will look after her if she needs it."

"You cannot want to discuss cats, can you?"

"Not especially, but I find I am not in a particular rush."

Tom asked again, pointedly, "Is it here?"

Instead of jibbing, Theo said, gazing steadily at him, "Yes."

"God, you really are something. If it were me, I'd want to escape into the sea as soon as I could. I'd want to be whole again. Benson said you would die if something happened to your. . ." Tom's head tilted slightly as he seemed to deliberate over what to call his skin. After a pause, the most direct word had won. "Skin."

"Escaping into the sea does seem to be your option of choice." Theo approved of his directness, but did not want to engage with the statement that he'd be whole with the skin. Though it was true in a literal, physical sense, he was realizing as they spoke that he was speaking to the thing that might complete him. Or, no, not complete him. That was dangerous and fanciful nonsense.

Tom offset him. Existing as counterweights was a much more fulfilling prospect than any idea of needing another to be complete.

Theo continued, "But if I did that, I couldn't talk to you. Seals are often tediously vocal, but we're not comprehensible to a man's ear. Hell, I don't even know what a seal's on about."

"Could you?"

"Could I what?"

"Die if your skin was. . . compromised." Tom sounded hollow, sad at the prospect.

Theo tried to soften the impact of his reply with a shrug and level tone. "Yes, as far as I know. Of course, I've never put it to the test and would prefer not to." The idea did not unnerve him as much as it did Tom, but only because he'd spent long enough getting used to it. It was still sobering, even more so now that he was in the same room with Tom again. He didn't want to die before they'd spent years together. Another person should not be one's sole reason to stay or go anywhere, but it certainly amazed him that he'd found someone who made him consider why he might choose to do either.

Tom did not lead or propel him to blindly *do* without stopping to feel as he did so.

Dropping like a smooth stone through still water, Tom sat down next to him. Their thighs touched, but the contact did not immediately galvanize Theo to claim him. Instead, his solid warmth felt restful and grounding. A thrum of need reverberated under that sense of calmness, but he told himself it was manageable. It wasn't, but it should be, so he told himself it was.

"Shit," Tom said. "Well, let's stop talking as though we're remarking upon the bloody weather or the day's work. We should find that skin and get it back to you, so you can—"

Now *that* was galvanizing.

There was so much he could say to it, should say to it.

It was what he'd longed to hear, but the most satisfying course seemed to be saying nothing and doing *something*. It was the contact, the closeness, but it was the words and how they roused such affection and gratitude, too. Theo half-twisted, and tenderly but insistently took Tom's face in his hands before he could tell himself not to do it.

Valiantly, Tom tried to finish his thought, which was praiseworthy and most likely necessary. But he was regarding Theo while he spoke and his look scorched and beseeched, though his words were somehow even. "You need it, though," he said. "If you have it back, you shall feel far less like you cannot—"

Palms still on his warm, unkempt cheeks, Theo kissed him full on the lips and did not discover what followed *cannot*.

∼

IF THEY HAD TRIED to rendezvous in the early days after he'd tried to drown, and kissed then, he might wonder if he'd actually died and gone to heaven instead of purgatory or hell. This was keen absolution and exultation together. But because it happened weeks later, he was aware he was gloriously alive. It was just as jarring as waking up with Theo's mouth on his after the cold had lulled him into oblivion, his lungs burning due to the seawater.

But this time, he was not seething, or in pain, or questioning why he'd been unsuccessful. He was luxuriating and questioning why they hadn't done this until now. Theo's hands were on his cheeks, then on either side of his throat with a caress, and finally came to rest on his shoulders.

An obvious answer to why they hadn't sluggishly surfaced through the pleasurable haze, and he inched back with a stuttering breath.

"Theo."

"Yes?" Theo followed him and crept forward, deepening instead of breaking the connection, and for a moment the answer sunk again. He clung to it as much as he was presently clinging to Theo, knowing if they transgressed certain boundaries they'd both feel distressed after the fact.

Perhaps long after the fact if just the way they kissed was any indication for what might come next. But nonetheless, he did not wish to set the stage for any kind of regret.

"Theo," he murmured.

"Like how you say my name." Clearly transfixed by what they were doing, Theo cleared his throat, and Tom felt a tremble of pride that he'd produced the reaction in such a striking man and in particular, this one.

"I don't know if now is the time." Even as he said it, he kissed the side of Theo's mouth.

"This feels very much like the time."

"It wouldn't be right, would it? And you said yourself you wouldn't make another exception for me. I'm not drowning." He closed his eyes as nimble fingers pressed a tense knot of muscles along his neck. "Believe me, suggesting a pause is taking every ounce of rational thought I have."

Maybe it should have mattered more that they were in another man's house without his permission or knowledge. Specifically another man who presently had a claim on one of them. Tom was disinclined to admit it, but he had a care for David in all of this.

What was more, he knew Theo did, too, or he would have absconded before now. Though it was rather masked by indecision and trepidation, some part of him must still care for David in one form or another. They might not be romantically suited, that much was apparent, but they likely cared for each other or the denouement of their relationship would have been much simpler.

Besides, Tom could understand a fear of change. His own fear of change was often what drove him to seek it, because it seemed more controllable if he instigated it himself.

"You have a good heart," said Theo.

He opened his eyes. "I think you do, too."

"Once I have talked to him," said Theo as his fingers worked at Tom's muscles, "promise me you'll reserve the room with the best view in The Shuck. But if you'd rather Norwich, I can think of a few places that are pretty and discreetly tucked away. Or we could venture north, too."

The implication that Theo was not simply going to run, or swim, off when he had what he wanted from the Mills' empty house was exhilarating. Tom wouldn't have blamed him if he chose to leave as soon as he could, particularly since he and David had been fettering out anyway, but it would have been crushing.

Still, I'd let you go. He did not say such a maudlin thing. "You think I'm going to let you watch the sea? Don't be daft."

"Well, it does seem you have a robust sense of honor under all your scowling and brooding." Theo chuckled and stroked both his hands lower, lower, until they were at his hips and under his coat, petting where his shirt was tucked in. "Maybe all you want to do is gaze at me and swoon at the sea."

"The sea doesn't make me swoon, but if your hands keep moving in that direction, you'll discover how *you* can," said Tom.

"Are you trying to encourage me, or stop me?"

"A little of both, I think."

Theo's hands finally stopped moving, he took a long breath as though preparing to dive, and looked up at Tom with so much fondness that Tom had to kiss him to show he reciprocated the feeling. Theo said, "One of us is very confused about what post-ponement means," but then he chuckled and scooted back on the chest so that they had a half-a-hand's width between them. "When I do talk to David, I shall be sure to tell him what pleasure I've forgone in the name of ethical behavior... and it's his fault."

"In some ways it might be his fault, but you're kinder than you say."

"I did love him once, or I thought I did. . . or I thought I could." Theo pinched the bridge of his nose. "I know hearts can change. I just didn't know mine had."

What about me? Tom wanted to ask, even though it was evident in the very air they were inhaling so close together. "When did you realize?"

"Oh, it should have been obvious to me when I went to check on you the morning after I met you. . . but I think it was clear that day I was all turned around and you helped me back."

"Poor David." After a pause, Tom said, "If you feel you can stand and move about, we should find you your skin." Resolutely, he had not touched anywhere that fell lower than a torso, so he was not about to ascertain with his own hands if Theo could walk without discomfort. He knew himself too well to think he could cleave to willpower if he did.

Rather pained, Theo said, "Do you think *you* can?"

Chuckling at how plaintive he sounded, he shrugged. "I wouldn't be able to if we carried on like this, but I'm trying to think about why I came here. What you need."

"Oh, I'll gladly tell you what I need."

Resisting the shiver that went through him, he stood and offered Theo a hand. "And I'll gladly listen when I have you to myself in my bed."

Theo entwined their fingers as he got to his feet, but when he was standing, he didn't let go of Tom's hand. Instead, he tugged him closer, into a promising embrace. He said, with his lips barely against Tom's left ear, "We'll see if you're able to last until *after* I'm done telling you. I don't think so, and the sight of this admirable control shattering shall be devastatingly gorgeous."

Open-mouthed as he listened and awash with anticipation, Tom believed him.

21

As many things in life were, the resolution to their quest was almost absurdly simple. There was no wicked witch, no dragon to slay, and no riddles to answer before they secured what they wanted. There was just a large, quotidian article of furniture to open.

Theo led Tom to the bedroom David now used when he came to stay, reasoning that they may as well look there. "I don't know if you found this to be true at all back when you knew him better, but he is remarkably prone to habit. Which isn't to say he's a dull lad, because truly he isn't. . . but I think it's worth it to. . ." he quieted when Tom squeezed his hand more sharply than might have been warranted to catch one's attention. "What?"

"As much as I don't want to see him as a villain and I don't. . . I do feel sorry for him. . . it's not my favorite thing to hear you talking well of him."

"So we're to extend sympathy and hold ourselves back from delicious sins of the flesh to avoid causing him undue pain, but you want me to talk as though I abhor him?" Theo grinned and looked over his shoulder.

"No, but. . . I can feel terrible for what his father was like and think he shouldn't have taken something that was yours."

"Oh, aye, that he shouldn't have. But what a complex lad you are."

"Never mind, sing his praises, I don't care," Tom said, raising his eyebrows. The corridor was darker than the rooms because it had no windows, but they'd been inside long enough for their expressions to be legible.

Theo chortled at Tom's face. "Anyway, what I meant to say was, he would always put scarves and things in the top drawer just here. They'd get rumpled or crushed, but he still persisted. I'd be remiss if I didn't just look." He pulled Tom inside the room and went to the armoire without letting his hand go.

"Fine."

It was difficult with one hand but he managed to open the doors, then pull on the smaller inner drawer just under the lowest shelf. "Well, fuck me, I should have known my mood was improving because I was getting nearer to the thing all along."

Without anything to mark it as special, there was his skin.

It was folded neatly, or as neatly as it could be since it wasn't exactly symmetrical, and that was all.

It could have been a pair of socks, or a muffler, or any piece of clothing one rarely thought about.

"Here I was telling myself your good humor was all due to me," said Tom from just behind him, wisely keeping enough distance so that their bodies did not touch. "But you can't be serious. Is it really just in the damn armoire?"

"It's really just in the damn armoire."

"What did he do, take it out of your trunk and

leave it here thinking you'd never notice or be too polite to say anything?"

Sighing as he touched the soft fur, Theo nodded.
"I think that's precisely what he did."

"He's absurd. What if you *had* said something?
What if you'd parted ways?"

"I don't know. But he wasn't happy with me after
that little encounter in the taproom, and he seemed to
hate how I had your gran's medal. I think he just took
something that wasn't his to relieve some of whatever
he felt. He never liked it. I didn't wear it out in public
so much, but the times I did. . . if he passed some remark. . . I just said it was a sentimental family thing
and I couldn't bear to part with it."

Tom clasped his fingers with his own, then relin-
quished them and put his hand on the small of Theo's
back. "I'd bet it's why he thought you were from
America."

He chuckled. "A little, probably. There are so many
trappers, and all. I just let him think it. . . but he never
did ask." It still stung mildly that David didn't know
where he'd come from, but he might be prepared to
say the lack of inquiry had most to do with David's
own woeful internal state. "It's a shame he didn't. I
could have taken him all manner of places where I
spent time as a young thing."

Tom was breathing on his neck in gentle puffs of
warm air that were comforting, not irksome. "I'm
sorry he never did."

"Thank you, but I think it has everything to do
with him and very little to do with me. On the other
hand, I didn't volunteer much about myself for fear it
would lead to deeper matters, ones I wasn't ready to
navigate with him. I suppose that didn't exactly encourage his curiosity, either."

"Can I ask. . . were you happy?"

Theo thought back and discovered he was, but regardless, he'd always felt like what he and David had was not enough. He said as much.

"We were, but it never felt properly aligned to me. It was never enough." He looked back at Tom, smiling with his eyes more than his mouth. "I'm sure there's some kind of nautical metaphor you could apply about breezes, and sailing, and difficulties. It was never so dire as a red sky at morning. I think, and I don't know if *he* would realize this, so much more goes on in his heart than he says—or allows to surface. Until he can contend with that, I don't know if lasting happiness is possible for him. Alone or otherwise."

Tom glanced from Theo's eyes to the skin he held. "If he knew his own heart better, he might not have done such a trite little stunt, hiding that."

Agreeably, Theo said, "In which case, I might have shown him more of mine, and he might have known what this was, *and* he might have left it alone. Or, who the hell knows, he might have kept it for himself."

But as he said it, he did not truly think it was so.

Neither, apparently, did Tom.

"I don't think he would have. I thought about that when Benson first told us. . . I wondered if David might have somehow suspected the truth of it all and acted maliciously." He sighed as though put upon to admit it. "But I didn't think he did, and more than that, I didn't think he's capable."

Breaking his own rule about beds, Theo sat on the edge of David's, feeling nothing particular at all about whose it was. He certainly was in a better state mentally and physically, but he was also bone-tired and couldn't blame himself for being exhausted. Idly, he petted at his skin and cast it gently to one side.

"God, I could sleep for a thousand years."

"Can you live that long?" Tom regarded him with one side of his mouth turned up.

"No, thank Christ and any of the saints you'd like to mention."

"How long do you live then? It has to be longer than others, doesn't it?"

"Why do you think so?" He stretched back on his elbows. "You've got it quite correct, but I want to hear why you've reached the conclusion before we've talked about it."

They had much to discuss, and Theo looked forward to drawing it out rather than declaring everything as though he'd been sent to a Catholic confessional to seek absolution.

"Well, it's simple. You don't look much older than I do, but you *behave* like one of those world-weary old men who sits around with his pipe. Sprightly, but philosophical as hell," said Tom, his little smirk changing into a fully smitten grin. "It's terrifying. Myself, I've spent the last five minutes with anger and fear jostling about in my head, and here's you coming out with 'much more goes on in his heart than he says' as though he only took your best pair of gloves. And did it by accident."

Theo yawned, and managed to say with a chuckle, "Oh, I *am* old. But gloves can be very dear."

Laughing, Tom said, "See what I mean? Costly, yes. But last I knew, gloves couldn't kill the man they belonged to." He sat next to Theo. "Or trap him at the will of who stole them."

"They used to poison royalty with gloves, you know."

"You're hopeless." He prodded Theo's shoulder.

"I'm exhausted, is what I am."

Tom looked at him with so much ardent trust that all the cares he possessed felt less pressing. At the moment, he knew he needed to address quite a few, and every last question concerned how to get from this state of life to a new one. Collectively, an enormous prospect. He hoped Tom was correct about his motivations and general perspective, for he would rather be judged philosophical than lacking in mettle.

"It would be in terribly poor taste to sleep here, not to mention illegal," said Tom.

"I don't know if I can force myself to stand."

"Very well," Tom said. "I shall stay up, you can rest, and we'll go back in an hour or two. Preferably before morning, because I don't trust that the caretaker is as docile as you think."

～

THEO HAD LEFT him a note that wasn't very long at all, saying unaccountably that something had come up and he needed to go to Cromer immediately. Even his usually neat handwriting looked harried.

It was in the most rancorous of spirits that David completed the journey by train the morning after the evening he'd seen the note, thankful he had no appointments and no other plans. He'd had to wait until then for service, for by the time he'd read the thing, it was too late to catch any trains at all. Theo managed to get the last one.

If this was his way of liaising with Tom, it would be woefully obvious, so David was somewhat cheered that he wasn't. Theo had more than enough stylish subtlety for all three combined and would never be so gauche.

Should one include Tom in that sum, it quite said

something, he thought peevishly as he looked up at
The Shuck's sign, a great wooden black dog swaying in
the breeze.

Even though he did not quite think the reason for
Theo being here was romantic or carnal, all his instincts said he should start at The Shuck and nowhere
else. Some bizarre thread connected them, fine and
golden like that damned old medal's chain. He swept
through to the taproom and looked about for Mr.
Apollyon.

A low fire spluttered in the hearth and someone's
teacup was on the table nearest the bar. He touched
the side of the cup gently to find it was still warm.

"Oh, good morning. Pardon me, we were just upstairs. If you'll be needing a room, let me check the
ledger," a woman said as she hurried into the room. "I
know we have a few that would serve, but one is being
tidied and one is near our, ah, loudest guest." She
straightened her dainty spectacles and offered David a
cheery smile after she'd had a moment to see him
properly.

He knew Mrs. Lloyd. They had been introduced
once, but years ago, and she did not recognize him.
"That won't be necessary. Is Mr. Apollyon about?"

"He is, but this may not be the one you're after,"
Mr. Paul Apollyon said from just behind Mrs. Lloyd.
He was neither friendly nor unfriendly as he spoke,
but he was definitely less inimical than Tom had been
when they'd last spoken in this taproom with Theo
between them like a dazed moderator trying to keep
track of a debate.

Unlike Mrs. Lloyd, Paul undoubtedly did recognize him and didn't look set to provide him with any
special favor.

"Good morning, Mr. Apollyon," said David, cautiously keeping to politeness.

"What brings you here? I wasn't given to believe your father, God rest him, approved of you or anyone spending time in public houses."

There was no way to make what he wanted to know sound like the usual sort of thing one would be in a public house for, so David said, "I am looking for my secretary."

"That would be Mr. Harper, correct?"

"Indeed."

"And why would he be here? If he's come to town, do you not have quite a wonderful house?"

There was that ancestral contrary streak. Taking a moment to secure some gravitas instead of letting all his ire show through, David said, "I don't know precisely why, and I don't know if he would be here."

"But you have come to ask after him."

"Yes," said David, feeling his cheeks going a little red. They were warm, but the air around him seemed bracingly cold, now. He attributed it to his imagination or some trick of his nerves. He'd been up all night, thinking about how much simpler his life would have been if Theo had not met Tom, had not pulled him from the sea. Everything could have gone to plan, then, and who knew, he might have found someone who suited him better than a jumped-up secretary from Leith.

Mrs. Lloyd sidled past her employer and procured the teacup on the table, deftly taking both it and its saucer without so much as a tinkle of bone china. Then she ventured through a doorway on the other side of the taproom, perhaps wisely sensing the tenor of conversation was not headed in a pleasant direction.

His words low, but strident, Mr. Apollyon said, "With respect, Mr. Mills, I don't give information on who is patronizing my establishment at any given time unless it is a police matter. Come back with an inspector, if you please. I suspect you're seeking knowledge that isn't yours in the first place."

Stunned by his temerity, David said, "Bold that you're calling it an establishment. I told Tom years ago I wished I could curse it, and perhaps I succeeded. It's not looking well, is it?" He looked around and knew he was harsh in his pronouncement, because nothing was in terrible repair. Everything was clean and in order.

If he was being charitable, he might call it well-loved, but he was being neither charitable nor fair-minded.

"David, stop. I wouldn't have left a note if I'd known you were going to harangue anyone in your path."

David turned to meet Theo's eyes. He'd come from the entryway, which meant he'd been in the common area or upstairs. That knowledge unexpectedly and swiftly crushed David's resolve, but not because he wished he'd been able to break things off with Theo before Theo could break things off with him. Somehow, it saddened him. "You. . . were here. . . all night?"

"No," said Theo.

The shadows under his eyes said otherwise, but David wanted to take him at his word. "Where else could you have been?"

After a wan smile, Theo said, "It's something of a tale. But I wasn't here all night."

"Please just tell me." David looked around at Mr. Apollyon, who lingered close to where Mrs. Lloyd had made her escape, only dimly aware that he was still present. Boldly, David thought, the man did meet his eyes, but there was an unexpected amount of compassion in them. It was much like what he read in Tom's expression when they'd briefly discussed his father's death, and as then, he didn't know if he appreciated it.

"Walk with me," said Theo, and he came to take his arm. "I need to speak with you. Should have done an age ago." Mute, watching him, David allowed him to grasp his coat and hook their elbows as though they were about to take a pleasant constitutional. Theo and Mr. Apollyon exchanged a meaningful look, the nature of which David couldn't discern. Then Theo was taking him out of the front door and back under the great black dog waggling in the wind. "You took something of mine. You ought not to have done it. I needed it back, but really. . ." he sighed. "I should start with other things. Just listen until the end, though."

For the first time since they'd first met, David vowed to hold his tongue and only listen.

~

WISELY, Tom felt, he stayed out of sight for the whole exchange. From one of the first floor windows, Benson's, in fact, he watched Theo and David go arm-in-arm toward the promenade. He and Benson had eavesdropped in the corridor leading to the kitchen and converted storeroom that Mrs. Lloyd kept as her bedroom, then rushed upstairs in a bid to see what direction Theo and David might take for their walk. He should have known the selkie would head for the sea.

The two of them made for a good picture, but it was too perfect. He turned away, confident in Theo and how he would tell David all that needed to be told.

Benson snapped his fingers and Tom looked at him askance. "Yes?"

"If he'd come here more often, I might have figured it out."

"Who?"

"Mr. Mills."

"Figured what out?" Puzzled, Tom sat on the spindly rattan chair by the window and yawned. True to his word, he'd remained awake while Theo took a few hours of rest, content to watch him as the light in the room changed, reluctant to wake him just before dawn so they could return to The Shuck without being caught by David's caretaker. Theo couldn't say for sure if he would make some kind of morning rounds, so they didn't want to risk it just to take a leisurely pace. "I would kill for some tea."

Benson extended his flask, which was full of absolutely-not-tea, and Tom shook his head. "That isn't tea."

"He's got it," said Benson. He returned his flask to an innermost pocket.

This succinct way of conversing was endearing and unique to him, but it was tiresome when one was working on so little sleep. Tom rested his elbow on the back of the chair and his chin on his palm, contorting in the diminutive seat. "If you could see your way to using longer sentences, I'd be most obliged."

"That Mills, he's got witchery talents."

Letting his eyes close for just a moment, too tired to be taken aback, Tom said, "You must be mistaken."

"Not at all. I've long suspected this place has been bewitched, and now I know."

"Bewitched? Don't be silly."

"Oh, you're going to argue that's silly?" Benson's grin was legible in his tone; Tom didn't have to open his eyes. "I know bewitchment and enchantment, sir, and believe you me, I know how to trace the threads of those who weave them. It's not enough of one to harm us all or cause any undue damage, but it's been enough to keep things a little dark and dreary and threadbare."

Only half-sold on the idea, Tom said, "And you think it's David who set it upon The Shuck?"

"Oh yes, I just saw the thread. Felt the thread. Feel it now. I need to decide how best to cut it. Sometimes that can hurt the person who cast it, even if they didn't mean to cast it in the first place."

"How in all the world would someone cast a curse without knowing it?"

"I didn't say it was a curse. Curses are a woeful business."

"Then, how would someone unknowingly *bewitch* anything?"

Benson made a sound between a snort and harrumph. "The better thing to ask is. . . if they can do it, how do they not? First thing I was taught was how to examine what I felt so that it didn't accidentally latch onto anything else and become an enchantment I didn't intend to set. And you heard him not ten minutes ago." He mimicked David's learned accent, splendidly successfully. "'I told Tom years ago I wished I could curse it.'"

At that, Tom opened his eyes. "He did. He was angry that I didn't think it was worth it to keep sneaking around to see him, and he just. . . snapped that he wished he could do something awful to The Shuck. Could curse it. We were here when he said it, and it was really the most obvious thing he could attack. But we all say ridiculous things as boys, don't we?"

"When some of us do, though, it might come true," Benson said.

Tom was loath to say so, but if he'd met anyone who was an expert at *not* examining what he felt, it was David. There was also all that babble about witch-hunting Mills that, once upon a time, David liked to repeat as one of his favorite family stories.

His other favorite was about Chocolate the rabbit, who took such a liking to his father that the little creature slept in a drawer in his bureau—his father reciprocated the sentiment so much that Chocolate was also allowed to hop at will in Mr. Mills' office unless appointments had been booked that day.

Perhaps due to the theme of his father loving something alive, David only ever told the story of Chocolate when he was very drunk. Tom got the sense David was both jealous of Chocolate and jealous of his father.

Chocolate had been a brown rabbit. Mr. Mills was not very creative.

"You're saying he's like you."

"Seems like he could be," said Benson, "if that faint green thread following him out the pub is an indication."

"Will you tell him?"

"Me tell him, who would look at me like I'm shit on the bottom of his best shoe?" Benson guffawed. "Well, I might, just to see how he'd react, but I don't want to do it today of all days."

Glancing at what little he could see of the sky from the way he'd settled in the chair, Tom thought of Theo, dreamily beginning to count down the hours until they could retire to his room. Of course, he might fall asleep before they could do anything very memorable, but he planned on having nights and nights with Theo ahead of him. "No, today isn't the day to tell him. He'll be adjusting his perspective enough without learning something so stark and new about himself."

"Who knows. It might not be so stark, once he's given time to reflect upon it. Might not even be new, neither, if he really thinks back on his experiences."

In all this, Tom had learned not to make as many assumptions about what he thought people were like inside their own minds. He just shrugged, yawned, and hoped that Theo would return soon.

~

THERE WAS something to be said for thorough pleasure that left him tingling with happy exhaustion. Theo looked up at Tom, who was flushed in the gloaming light and had shattered under the weight of sinuous, suggestive words just as he'd predicted.

"Really," Tom said. "Are you sure you're all right?"

"Yes," said Theo, serenely curling his fingers into some hair at the nape of Tom's neck.

"Don't try to distract me again."

"I wasn't trying half an hour ago, either. And the last person I want to talk about while I'm in your bed is David."

"Well, I don't want to talk about him, either, but he *knows* now."

"And I told you, he was appalled at what he'd done."

"You don't think he'll try to. . ."

"What, dear heart, exact revenge?" Theo shook his head. "There is nothing between us that would merit that kind of thing. The only thing that shocked him was what I am, not what I planned to do. He confessed he had been thinking of how to tell me he didn't want to carry on. Sometimes these things fall apart mutually."

Quiet, Tom took a deep breath and Theo's head rose, then drifted back down, with his chest. It was with great delight that he'd confirmed how wiry Tom actually was. "I can't say why. . . with any rational evidence. . . but he feels trustworthy. Even when we fell out, he never felt duplicitous, just angry and hurt."

"I do think he's learned not to take things that aren't his, and if it does worry you that he'll start any blether about selkies. . . don't be worried. His clientele is the pinnacle of no-nonsense, remember. It would make him look absurd, and he'd hate that." He kissed the hollow of Tom's throat. "I haven't any reason to believe he's malicious. Why, when I explained we hadn't spent the night together in any scandalous sense, he was cheered."

Theo heard the scowl in Tom's voice. "So he didn't cherish you, really, and didn't want you, really, but it would have been a crushing blow if we'd done anything? I can't understand him."

"Thankfully, you don't need to. It's finished."

"Is it?"

"Do you know something I don't?"

"Well," Tom said, stroking a trail with his pointer finger along Theo's spine, "Benson noted something as you were both walking out. We'll have to hear it from him to know entirely what he's on about, and we might need my uncle to chivvy him along to making sense, but he thinks David *bewitched* The Shuck."

"That is rather unexpected," said Theo, arching his back into Tom's fingertip. "So much so, I believe it."

"I'm not sure if I do."

"I think you don't want to."

The fingertip turned into the barest hint of a fingernail, and Theo gasped silently. Tom said, "I don't, but mostly for his sake. He's already had to think about you being not what he thought, and now he has to think about himself being not what he thought?"

"But such is life for us all, and is that proper empathy for *David* I hear creeping into your voice?"

Firm hands settled on his waist as Tom said, "Not in the least."

"I think it is," said Theo. "Heart of gold, you've got."

"Tell no one."

"But I love it."

"I'd rather hate the world."

"No, you wouldn't," said Theo tranquilly. "I think you secretly want to keep an eye on him, and not because you think he'll harm me."

Looking down at him from the close distance, Tom said, "If he did, there'd be hell to pay." He gently kissed the top of Theo's head.

They kept quiet for some minutes before Theo said, idly speculating if Tom had fallen asleep, "I love you for both. The hell you'd give *and* the way you want to help."

"Truly?" was his astonished, small rejoinder. "You love me."

"Oh, yes." Contented, Theo yawned. "Sorry, I'm still a bit tired after everything. . . just give me the rest of your life, and I'll do all I can to show you I'm deeply in earnest. Once that's finished, I'll emulate you and disappear into the sea."

EPILOGUE
AFTER BELTANE, 1901

All manner of thing shall be well.

— MOTHER JULIAN OF NORWICH

In the end, Tom admitted it was a blessing that Benson was descended from witch-hunters and had been trained by his parents, who'd been trained by their parents, because once it was all out in the open—David's unintentional, mild bewitching of The Shuck and consequently, anyone in it, and Theo's identity—Benson really could remedy a lot of their collective troubles.

It seemed "witch-hunter" actually meant "witch who protects witches who don't actively want to harm anybody, and also jaunty selkies who get themselves into a spot of bother with a witch who doesn't quite know they're a witch but might accidentally bewitch something."

Heaven forbid, though, anyone insinuate Benson was in essence more of a witch than anything else. It was not that he hated witches and only that he didn't want to claim the title when his forebearers hadn't suffered for bearing it. According to him, witch-hunters of the twentieth century were more like witch-protectors. But if Tom had learned anything from him at all in recent months, it was that protecting was better on the soul than hunting, yet there was always an element of pursuing to defending.

Walking down the stairs and into the entryway brought him to what felt like an entirely different establishment in comparison to the momentous December when he'd wanted to try his hand at dying. Tom took a breath and loved the breeze that played against his skin.

But it wasn't only that Mrs. Lloyd had just opened the windows to admit a gray day's air. Benson had put all sorts of sigils on The Shuck that curtailed malicious gossip, ensured good business, and made it easier for Tom to experience whatever anyone came in feeling. He also somewhat lessened David's unintentional jinx on the place, but they were still attempting to figure out how to lift it entirely without harming David.

Meanwhile, Benson's habitual addled persona did not disappear entirely, for it seemed he did enjoy shocking newcomers, but it mellowed considerably after their shared adventures. Even with all his arcane knowledge, he was nothing more than a friend, just as Theo was nothing more than a man whose face belied his years. At least, Tom chose to see things that way. He was no philosopher or scholar capable of unraveling the implications of myths.

Theo would say he was a romantic, but he wasn't sure if he was one of those, either.

He was, though, happy. Months on from stealing his selkie's skin only to give it back, his mind was clear, his heart was content, and for the first time he could remember, he looked forward as well as inward.

The inky days still came and he did not know if they'd cease to come.

Sometimes many of them in a row came, and Theo was patient, willing to wait out the ink until Tom surfaced again. They were also planning a way for him to become less reliant on drink, but until they decided on a firm strategy, he was still partaking a little. More than other men, perhaps, but far less than he had previously and always without the relentless need to be deadened to the world.

There was much they could accomplish together, but there was no need to rush and certainly no advisable way to rush these large changes. Much like David was probably not ready to embrace his own preternatural abilities, having just come to terms with a selkie —and no one was sure how to encourage him to go about it—Tom was not yet able to live his life so differently. The ability would come, he was sure. His change in perception was not as difficult as the physical realities of changing his habits, and he found he did not need much time to adjust to how well his life had become. With that had come his better outlook.

Today was not an inky day, though it was possibly going to be a somber one by virtue of what Theo had located with the help of some old newspapers and corroborated with civic records.

If Paul was not too occupied with the grocer who chattered away at him outside the kitchen, or with the carpenter who was coming to repair some wood paneling on the stairs, Theo was going to tell him where he could visit Alistair.

The advantage to being a seal when one traveled to Scotland, or so Tom was told, was the travel itself did not require transport or room and board in the conventional sense and one could spend one's days exploring mundane, dull trifles like timeworn papers and cemetery records.

He'd found Alistair with little more than a date of birth, date of interment, and surname. It helped that Alistair's son had buried his father where he was born, which was to say near Portobello, but Tom was impressed Theo could do such a thing so expediently.

Theo demurred, claiming he'd had plenty of practice tracking people down for the purposes of sending invoices and various pieces of correspondence and the like. Still, Tom doubted he'd have the patience or even know where to look for such information himself.

Theo said he'd look after The Shuck in the event both its proper landlords ventured away to visit a grave, and Tom trusted him more than anybody to keep his word.

The days were full of work especially now that summer dawned. Sometimes it was work that left both of them cantankerous and exhausted in the cottage Theo bought, and they shared, so Paul could keep his flat. But the nights were theirs, whether to explore each other with touch and the exchange of words, or simply to sleep side by side, occasionally with Theo falling asleep and laying diagonally. That meant Tom had to creep in the dark to one of the wingbacks he'd pilfered from The Shuck if he wanted any space at all for proper rest. He didn't mind.

In his version of the myth about a man who stole a selkie's skin, the selkie kept the man.

And right now, clutching handwritten notes that detailed the way for yet another man to find where his heart had gone, his smiling selkie crossed into the entryway to meet him.

ALSO BY CAMILLE DUPLESSIS

Coming Soon

The Only Story

Unfair Winds

ABOUT THE AUTHOR

Camille is a thalassophile who sadly spent too long residing in Chicago, where there's just a very large lake and no sea. An enquiring and possibly over-educated mind, she's been described as "the politest contrarian." Though everyone believes she's tall, she's not. Likewise, she doesn't dress in all-black.

f